WILD LIKE US

Willow River Press is an imprint of Between the Lines Publishing. The Willow River Press name and logo are trademarks of Between the Lines Publishing.

Between the Lines Publishing
1769 Lexington Ave N, Ste 286
Roseville MN 55113
btwnthelines.com

First Published: June 2023

ISBN: (Paperback) 978-1-958901-27-4

ISBN: (Ebook) 978-1-958901-28-1

WILD LIKE US

Jennifer Liss

For Samuel and Abel

CHAPTER 1

Naomi scrambled up a tree, plucked an avocado—firm, black, and cratered—and jumped back to the thin mat. With her pocketknife, she slit the fruit in two, popped out the seed with one flick, and sliced out big, soft chunks, which she dropped, right off the blade, into Lu's open mouth. The girls' work in the Crisis Camp orchard was done for the day.

Lu's eyes were big gray globes. When Naomi looked at them directly, she felt like the skittish feral cat who hung around the outskirts of the orchard, near the high wall where the Hirelings patrolled.

"It's 'cause you have a crush on her," Shay had said when Naomi confided in her about the feeling. "Should tell her already. Get it over with. Make you feel less jumpy."

That was every day, all day, in the dry heat, in the orchard, or during the foggy, starless nights in their tent in the secured girls' Crisis Camp run by Headquarters high up in the canyon. Naomi was always thinking about Lu's eyes and the weird feelings she had, which she could not stop or make sense of.

The siren made the girls sit up. Naomi ditched the avocado. They popped to their feet and galloped wordlessly down the hill to the big open tent where they ate and played card games and listened to lectures about the Crisis and why Headquarters had erased their memories.

A Headquarter's Director was there with two Hirelings. The Director's frizzy red hair snuck out from beneath her green cap and sweat shimmered above her top lip. The girls whispered and fidgeted. It was rare for a Director to have an announcement.

Lu stood close to Naomi, almost leaning against her. Naomi could hear her breath whistle through the big space between her two top front teeth.

"Girls, listen up," the Director said in a dry, tired voice. "Canyon Region Headquarters has passed a new law." She pulled out a crumpled piece of paper from her pocket and read from it.

"The Memory Restoration Act for the Children of the Crisis Camps."

She shoved the paper back into her pocket. Then the Director gave a long speech, sometimes looking at the girls, but often looking over their heads, out the big tent opening into the Crisis Camp orchard where they worked.

"When the Crisis was at its worst, when everything in the Canyon Region was completely falling apart, when there wasn't enough food, when Wilds roamed the streets terrorizing everyone—you came here. Here, at the Crisis Camp, we could give you work, food, and safety. Your families were struggling, and although they wanted to, they couldn't take care of you. Of course, it was hard for them. But eventually, they let you go."

The Director's voice had become hollow and small, as if she was talking to herself. It occurred to Naomi that the Director could still remember what it was like when families who had once worked for Headquarters and had lived comfortable lives, fled on trains and boats for other Regions, as daily life in the Canyon Region was being ripped apart.

The Director still had her memories. Naomi didn't. For a moment, she felt bad for her.

The Director rubbed her eyes and continued. "For your health, we gave you a drug that erased your memory so you wouldn't have to remember any of the Crisis. So you wouldn't have to remember all the horrors of that time. You know all this because we've told you."

She waved her hand absentmindedly, wiped the sweat from her lip, and shoved loose, frizzy curls back into her cap.

"You were just girls. You *are* girls. Here you are able to work in the orchards in peace, to live your childhoods in peace." Again, the Director looked past the girls, out into the land, as if she was considering the word "peace" for the first time.

"There are new leaders at Headquarters now with new ideas. They say everyone has a right to their memory—as horrible as it might be—so they passed this new law. You can have your memory back. Understand? You get to choose. It's your *right* now."

She took the paper out of her pocket again and waved it. "A doctor will be in the tent tomorrow at dawn. If you want your memory back, be there. He won't stay long."

The Director turned to leave but then swung back. "Another thing. If you choose to take your memory back, you can no longer stay here. Your memories will affect you and everyone else. We can't have that. If you choose your memory, we will immediately remove you from the camp. You'll go back into the Crisis."

CHAPTER 2

Naomi sat in the open entryway of their tent with her knees hugged tightly to her chest. Lu's head was in Shay's lap, and Shay played with Lu's dusty hair.

"Well?" Lu asked.

"Not me. I'm not doing it," Shay said. "You know what it's like out there? Madness. I'm not leaving the camp. I don't need my memories. What good are they anyway?"

"How do you know what it's like out there?" Naomi asked.

Shay twisted a curl on Lu's head. "You've seen the pictures. You've heard the stories. Headquarters has told us. I don't want to starve or have to always be looking over my shoulder to see if some Wild is coming to get me. I don't want to be scared all the time."

"But don't you want to know for yourself?" Naomi pressed.

Shay sighed. "Naomi, you're *too* curious. It's not good for you. I've been telling you that. It's like all your questions about the moon. Too many questions. Too much wondering. Right, Lu?"

Lu clucked in agreement.

Naomi stared up at the taut canvas of the tent ceiling. Headquarters was always telling them that curiosity caused restlessness, not peace. But Naomi couldn't help but wonder.

Take the moon for example. It was brighter than all the other stars in the night sky. Why? Was it even a star, or something else entirely? Why was it sometimes swollen and full and sometimes thin, like the clipping of a fingernail? What purpose did it serve? The sun clearly provided warmth. But the moon? Did it keep the night cool? How far away was it? Had anyone ever been there?

Shay and Lu had agreed with Naomi that they likely had known the answers to these questions when they lived outside of camp, in the Crisis. But unlike Naomi, the girls didn't worry about the answers now.

Shay continued. "Listen. Our families have probably all fled–or worse. Nothing is the same. Nothing! No stores. No school. You'll be alone there.

How will you take care of yourself? Where will you go? What will you do? It will be *so* hard. It's too scary to even think about."

"Not if we all go," Naomi said. "We'll be together."

She allowed herself to steal a glance at Lu, whose eyes were closed.

"I don't remember anything," Lu said. "There's no part of me that wants to. No desire to remember. I have a *feeling* my memories are even worse than they say. It feels weird to say this, but I have a feeling that I am supposed to be here."

Lu sat up and patted the dusty floor of the tent, emphasizing *here*.

"Me too," Shay nodded. "It's not good out there. I just know it."

"But what about here? What's going to happen to us here? We're just going to work in the orchard forever?" Naomi asked. "Is that all you really want to do?" Her voice sounded whinier and thinner than she intended.

Neither Shay nor Lu responded. Naomi rolled around the small silver ball that was in her pocket.

Sometimes, after Lu and Shay fell asleep, after the fog had infiltrated the Crisis Camp, creeping up the canyon from the wide, violent ocean—which Naomi knew was out there but couldn't remember—Naomi felt a pull. It was like someone grabbed a fistful of her shirt, tugging so hard that the shirt stretched and lost its shape immediately. *Come.* That's the word she heard in her mind. *Come.*

She had never told Shay or Lu about the pull. She could barely string the words together to even describe it.

The feeling had started after Naomi found the small silver ball. She was raking leaves in the orchard, when it caught her eye, a shiny speck in the caked dirt under the leaves. She used a sharp branch to dig it out and spat on it to clean it off. A long time ago, the ranch had been owned by a family. She figured the ball had been left out there, many years ago, buried with time. Either that or one of the Hirelings had dropped it while they patrolled the rows.

Since then, she had developed a habit of rolling it around in her pocket between her thumb and index finger. Something about the ball—its size and shape and surprisingly heavy weight—was familiar to her, and ever since she found it, she began to experience the pull, which she suspected may have been there all along, but that she simply hadn't noticed.

She hadn't told Shay or Lu about any of it. Instead, she fought the pull silently on the inside, while striving to be a good friend and a strong, steady worker on the outside.

"Are you seriously going to leave us?" Lu asked Naomi. "That's crazy. You're too much, Naomi."

Shay didn't give Naomi a chance to respond. "Naomi is too loyal. She loves us too much to leave. We're her family now."

All that night, Naomi lay awake listening to Lu snore lightly and Shay toss and turn. Once the sky turned an end-of-night gray, she laced her boots. *Come.* The word had been a steady holler in her mind all night, but as she made her way toward the big tent, rolling the ball in her pocket, the holler sounded less demanding and more inviting. The moon dipped low on the western horizon, its fullest shape, perfectly round.

Naomi took that as a sign that she was doing the right thing.

CHAPTER 3

Nobody came. In the entrance of the big tent, Naomi paused. She expected to see other girls emerge from the fog. But she was the only one.

Inside, the doctor sat next to an empty cot. The Director wasn't there. Hirelings weren't there.

The doctor raised his eyebrows and tilted his head to one side. He looked as surprised to see Naomi as she was to be the only one. The smell of last night's dinner lingered in the tent.

Suddenly, Naomi felt small. This was a serious situation. A serious decision. She was sure she had made consequential decisions before—in her old life, before she came to the camp. But those memories were gone. How was it done? How was she supposed to go about deciding something that would affect the rest of her life?

Since arriving at the Crisis Camp and having her memory stripped, the only real decision Naomi had to make was whether to tell Lu that she might have a crush on her. And she couldn't even make that decision. Every aspect of her life was now controlled. She had been assigned to a tent with Shay and Lu. The Director told them when to work, eat, and rest. Hirelings told them what they needed to know about life outside the Crisis Camp. Everything had been just fine.

A desire to race back to her tent and to her sleeping friends made Naomi catch her breath. She rolled the ball around in her pocket, and somehow she moved forward, toward the cot and the doctor with the raised eyebrows.

"Memory restoration?" the doctor asked.

"Yes," she said quietly and laid down on the cot.

The doctor picked a syringe off the tray. Up close, she could see the deep lines in his face. The puffy skin under his eyes. The few adults she'd seen in the Crisis Camp had a similar look—exhausted, vacant.

"Memories will come back in waves," he explained. "You will know about your past, but not all of it, not all at once. Some memories will be stronger than others. Strong ones might repeat. You might see something—or smell something—that will trigger a new one. But you will wake up with enough memories to have a general sense of who you are and where you came from."

Involuntarily, Naomi's left leg began to shake. She took deep breaths to try to steady it.

Suddenly, the doctor lunged toward her. Before she could react, his lips were next to her ear whispering roughly. "Head down the canyon. Be alert. Trust your memories. *Trust your memories.* Avoid people in the canyon. Town is on the coast. Get to town. *Get to town.* Don't come back."

Before she could respond, he yanked up her sleeve and plunged the syringe into Naomi's arm.

CHAPTER 4

Papa charges into the waves with Naomi in his arms. Over Papa's shoulder, she sees Mama on the beach. Eli rests on Mama's hip. He howls with laughter as Papa throws Naomi into the warm, frothy waves.

Sunlight washes over Naomi's bed. Mama peels back the covers. "Out east there's a city with bridges like clouds and roads like rivers and towers like trees. Come with me love, to the city out east. Sprinkle glitter in your hair, love, and come with me to the city out east," Mama sings. It's an old song, and the way Mama sings it makes Naomi wish she could live in another time.

"What's glitter, Mama?"

Mama shakes her head the way she does when they talk about something from the past. "It sparkles," Mama *explains. "Like sunlight on water. It's tiny, tiny, tiny pieces. Like sand."*

"Can we get glitter?" Naomi asks.

"There's no more glitter," Mama says.

Mama sits on the kitchen counter. Papa stands in front of her. Mama's legs are wrapped around his waist. He rubs his beard against her cheek and whispers in her ear. Tears spill from Mama's eyes.

"Are you happy crying?" Eli asks, and Mama nods yes, and Eli and Naomi try to shove their way in between Mama and Papa to get in on the crying-laughing hug, but Mama and Papa start kissing and squeeze themselves tight together and Eli and Naomi can't pry them apart.

Naomi found herself on her hands and knees, struggling to breathe. Her own tears seemed to be choking her, pouring from her eyes straight into her mouth, down her throat, flooding her insides. She rocked back and forth. Drool and snot dripped from her face onto the dusty, dry leaves on the ground.

She could hear someone wailing, calling the name "Eli" over and over. Then she realized the sound was coming from her. She was crying out for him, her brother. Her baby brother.

What had she done? What ridiculous, stupid decision had she made? In the Crisis Camp, she had never suffered except for the dumb, itchy feeling she had about whether to tell Lu she had a crush on her.

That wasn't suffering. That wasn't a problem. That was peace.

Now, she was outside the Crisis Camp, alone except for her memories—fully aware that she came from a family who loved her and who were probably gone, long gone. What had she done? Why hadn't she listened to Shay? Shay had warned her so explicitly to stay in the camp, and yet, Naomi hadn't listened. Shay was right. She was crazy.

Her mind raced to take stock of what had happened. She had gone to the big tent, willingly, and made the choice to restore her memory. After the doctor gave her the shot, she passed out. When she woke up, she wasn't in the Crisis Camp anymore, but she was still in the canyon, miles from town. She was on the side of the main road, which she had traveled many times with her family, before the Crisis. Ranchers had lived up this way. Were they still here? Rich people, people with strong ties to Headquarters, had owned spacious homes around this area, too. Were they gone also?

She sat up on her knees in the shade of an ancient oak tree, surrounded by golden grass.

Naomi stopped crying, steadied her breath, closed her eyes, and tried to let the memories fill her up with more missing information.

A startling realization became clear to her: when she was taken to the girls' Crisis Camp, Eli was *not* taken to the boys' Crisis Camp. She knew this like she knew other indisputable facts about herself, like that she had ten fingers, and her name was Naomi and she had been born and raised in the Canyon Region.

Naomi squeezed her hands into fists, willing more memories to present themselves. If her parents couldn't take care of their children, if the Crisis had left them foodless or homeless like it had so many others, why did they abandon her but not Eli?

It didn't make sense. She didn't have access to the right memories to answer the question. But she was certain—the doctor had said to trust the memories, hadn't he?—that Eli wasn't in a camp.

Instead of answers, she heard Mama's voice in her mind singing the words to the old song about the city and the glitter, and it made her sob again.

CHAPTER 5

"Watch your brother," Mama says, so Naomi does, as he crawls like a crab across the hot sand, straight toward the sea.

She jumps in front of him, making him giggle from the surprise.

"Where are you going, silly boy?" Naomi says. "You can't swim. You can't even walk! You have no business in the water."

She scoops him up to carry him back to Mama. This makes Eli mad, and he thrashes around in her arms.

"Down!" he demands, although the word sounds like, "dah."

"If I put you down," Naomi warns. "You can't crawl back toward the sea."

She sets him on the sand, and Eli giggles with delight, wasting no time to gallop, on hands and knees, back toward the frothy waves.

Naomi lay back down on the dry leaves, tracing the outline of the twisty oak branches with her mind's eye. She had cried herself into a stillness, a floating feeling she remembered from being a little girl after a tantrum.

Now, she was animal alert. She realized that a backpack was next to her. Whoever had escorted her out of the camp and deposited her in the grove of oak trees must have left it for her. Inside it, she found several canisters of water, food packets, and a change of clothes. There was even a thin blanket, rolled tightly.

She searched her pockets for her pocketknife, but it was gone. In camp, the knife was for work, and she never considered using it for anything else. Now, Naomi wished she had it.

With the newly awakened vigilance, next steps came to her with clarity and urgency: get out of the canyon, get to town, find Mama, Papa, and Eli.

Naomi walked into the center of the road, looking for a sign of how far she was from town. Once, the road had been used by ordinary people, like her family, who owned cars. But that was long before the Crisis, before she was even born. Now only the rich people at Headquarters drove cars and trucks. Her family used Heliarides, a type of motorbike that ran on electric and solar power. Naomi saw an old yellow road marker: Canyon Region Outpost #5–0.5 miles.

Outpost #5 was a shopping center with a hardware store and a café that sold mostly donuts, but sometimes sweet and spicy soup in the winter or on cool days. On her parents' day off, Naomi's family would often come up the canyon on their Heliarides to go to the café. It was a treat. The memory of the café consumed Naomi. She could smell it—meat and cloves and mint and sugary baked goods.

The café could not have survived the Crisis. But what if it had? *What if?* What if all she had to do was walk half a mile down the road and a steaming bowl of noodles with perfectly cut jalapenos *and* a pink glazed donut were waiting for her?

Motivated by the memory, Naomi quickly strapped on the backpack and headed down the road, toward the shopping center, on the way to town where her family lived—or had once lived.

The lone sound of her boots crunching on the gravel rang in Naomi's ears. She fought to stay calm. As a distraction, she allowed herself to think of Lu. She imagined Shay and Lu waking to her empty cot. All the girls would be talking, surely. They had been offered one chance to reclaim their memories and only Naomi took it. Would Lu be proud?

Heartbroken? She imagined Shay wrapping her arms around Lu, as they cried.

Naomi would become their first new memory of loss.

Something crashed through the brush, and instinctively Naomi crouched down, her arms spread out like wings. A coyote stepped out of the manzanitas and onto the road.

Both the animal and Naomi eyed one another. Coyote howls were a familiar night sound in the camp. They were shy animals that usually avoided humans, but still, they were common residents of the Canyon Region, and Naomi and the other girls had seen several of them, prowling the orchard for food. Coyotes were actually welcome on the land, since they helped keep the pest population under control. The ones Naomi had seen had thick, grayish- brown fur, skinny legs, large ears, and ochre eyes. They were crepuscular animals, active around dawn and dusk. For that reason, it unsettled Naomi to see one in the morning sun.

The coyote averted its eyes and dropped its head, a gesture that Naomi instinctively recognized as submission. This too seemed strange. She took in the animal, noticing other particularities. Its eyes were dark, so black they were almost blue. It was smaller than the other coyotes she'd seen. Most surprising, a frayed collar made from tattered rope hung loosely around its neck.

It all came together. This was a coyote-dog, bred from a male coyote and a female dog, and had likely once been someone's pet. Naomi figured that the owner was long gone, if not dead. She squatted and held out her hand. The coyote-dog touched its nose to her palm and then rubbed its muzzle against her leg. "Good dog," Naomi said. "Sweet dog."

Its tail wagged, and Naomi sat on the road so it could circle and smell her, know her. Naomi wanted to call the dog something. "Lu," she whispered but nothing about that name seemed right.

Lu was behind her, part of her memories.

"Glitter," Naomi said to the dog, hearing Mama's singing voice in her mind. She liked the way saying the word made the corners of her mouth naturally turn up into a smile.

CHAPTER 6

Eli is tucked into Mama's backpack. His sweaty, pink face rests at the nape of her neck. Naomi trudges behind Mama, jealous of sleeping Eli being carried. Her legs grow heavier with each step. They had picked up the trail in the open wilderness behind Naomi's favorite donut shop. But now they had been hiking too long, too far.

"Almost there," Mama had said so many times that Naomi didn't believe her anymore. Mama says hiking in the canyon is good for them, but Naomi wishes they would have gone to the donut shop first, with the loud box fan, the sticky floors, and the sweet woman in the stained apron who gave her free donut holes.

"Know the features of the land. Don't just look, but notice," she says as she walks. "Understand. Naomi, you have to always pay attention."

She points to a flowering artichoke plant on the side of the trail. With its spiky leaves and otherworldly purple flowers, it looks wild, yet normal, a thriving plant in the Canyon Region.

Mama rattles a leaf, and the plant explodes with thousands of ants and aphids, driving in and out of the flower. "See? Everything seems fine, but it's not. Infested! Don't assume anything is what you think it is. You have to notice."

It seems like Mama is talking to herself. Not that it matters. Naomi is barely listening, resisting the urge to complain. There is a rock in her shoe, her mouth is sticky and dry, and the sun is beating down on the top of her head. Sure, Mama had said to bring a hat and Naomi had refused, but still. All she can think about is donuts.

Just as Naomi is about to stop, sit in the dirt, and refuse to move, Mama says, "We're here!" and points to a cool, granite cave, carved into the side of a cliff. Mama unstraps the pack and carefully lowers Eli to the ground. He moans and his head rolls from side-to-side against the back of the pack, before he nods back to sleep. Naomi peers into the dark cave, which smells stale.

"Mama, I think it's a mountain lion den," Naomi says.

"Why?" Mama asks.

"Cause," Naomi says. She doesn't actually think it is a den, but she wants to compel Mama to leave, to go back down the trail that leads to sweet, pink frosted

donuts. Mountain lions can be dangerous. Maybe this will make Mama change her mind.

"It's a good place to know about," Mama says. "You know, in case, you need to go somewhere." Naomi is confused. Why would she go somewhere? Why would she leave Mama? Now it is Naomi's turn to ask Mama what she means.

"I don't know," Mama says quietly. "Things are starting to change." Naomi sits in Mama's lap, presses her head against Mama's chest and feels her heartbeat. Mama kisses the top of her head and sighs.

"Never mind, sweet girl," Mama says. "You're right. It's probably a mountain lion den. We should go before she gets back. Also, let's get home before Papa gets home from work. Snack first?"

Naomi nods, and Mama pulls oranges from her pack. The slices are juicy and tart, perfect. "Yum," Naomi says. "So tasty."

When the memory faded, Naomi was surprised to find the coyote-dog lying next to her, its haunches folded neatly underneath it. "Glitter," she called to the animal, who didn't respond, but when she rose to her feet, its ears perked up. She began to walk, and the coyote-dog followed her, down the road, through the canyon.

Soon the road widened into an empty intersection with a dead stoplight. Naomi stood in the middle of it. Ahead was Outpost #5.

She walked through the neglected parking lot to the café window, shattered into hundreds of small, jagged pieces. Inside, the donut case was smashed, too. On the sidewalk, in front of the café, was a spray-painted blue "W," the symbol of the Wilds. The Director had shown the girls pictures of this symbol, plastered on buildings and homes.

Naomi gulped down her disappointment. Nothing was as she remembered it. Glitter sniffed around the cracked sidewalk. The tough pads of its feet undisturbed by the broken glass.

Getting to town, that was the most important thing. She had to focus on that. Yet there was another distraction: the cave memory. It had come back to her quickly for a reason. She felt sure of it. The doctor had said to go into town, but he didn't know Naomi's family. He didn't know how resourceful they could be.

Naomi clicked her tongue at Glitter, and the animal began to trot after her. Just behind Outpost #5 and the donut shop, they made their way to the trailhead, overgrown now with rough-leaved bushes and sharp vines. The animal slid to a place in front of her, and she followed behind, watching its bushy tail collect burs as they went. As they moved single-file through the thick vegetation, Naomi could hear Mama's voice from that day in her mind, advising her on things that had made no sense at the time. Quails flitted across the trail, diving into the bushes on the other side. Naomi and the coyote-dog kept on.

Naomi was older now and stronger, from many months of agricultural work in the Camp, so before long, before she and Glitter reached a small clearing in front of the cave. The hike hadn't taken as long as she remembered it on that day with the artichoke flower. Just as she hoped, there *were* signs of human activity. A short metal drum was full of charred bits of wood, which had clearly been used for a fire. Even more promising was a woman's sandal, with a dirty pink strap and a broken buckle. Naomi stared at it, trying to conjure a memory. Did Mama have a shoe like that? There was also a filthy sweatshirt. It was plain blue with dark stains. Just looking at it made Naomi uncomfortable, but she nudged it with her toes, hoping it would trigger a memory. Yet, like the sandal, the sweatshirt meant nothing to her.

"Hello?"

Nobody but Glitter responded. The coyote-dog paced in front of her, head lowered.

"What is it?" she asked the animal, keeping her eyes on the cave entrance.

The coyote-dog's ears stiffened.

"Mama?" Naomi called out, eyes fixed on the dark opening of the cave. She stepped toward the entrance, hesitating.

"Is anyone here?"

Naomi's voice was met with a moment of heavy silence and then shattered by Glitter's bark. The coyote-dog tipped its head back and barked ferociously, scaring Naomi so thoroughly that her breath felt trapped in her throat.

Glitter ran away, in the opposite direction of the trail, through an overgrown patch of poison oak and disappeared into the wilderness.

Alone, Naomi tried to steady herself and notice something, anything, that might reveal whether Mama and her family had been at the cave. But there was only a screaming siren inside her mind, triggered by the animal's bark and sudden departure.

"Glitter! Let's go!" She tried to beckon the coyote-dog back, but it was gone. Worried by what Glitter might have seen or sensed, she didn't wait a moment longer before turning around, and quickly returning to Outpost #5.

Back in the abandoned shopping center, Naomi caught her breath. Going to the cave had been a reckless idea. Of course, Mama wasn't there. Why would she have brought her family to a shallow cave? Naomi scolded herself. Not only had going there been dangerous, but the misstep had caused her to lose a companion too. It would have been safer to have Glitter with her. Now she was alone, again. From here on out, she promised herself she would make better decisions.

Naomi moved swiftly through Outpost #5, heading back to the road, which she should have never strayed from. Her mission was simple. Get to town.

But before she could move forward, a light refraction caught her eye. In the broken glass, Naomi saw fragments of her reflection. She hadn't seen herself since she had been in the Crisis Camp. The tents all had screens, no windows.

Now, she could see her long black hair tangled at her scalp, yet smoother as it flowed down her back. Her shoulders had broadened from the work she'd done in the orchard.

Naomi could see her father in the shape that her body was becoming: slender but strong. Her skin looked rough and scaly, weathered from working in the sun and enduring the cycles of sunburns and healing. Her father's skin was a light pink, and her mother's was a reddish-brown, the color of a hawk. Naomi and Eli had always been a creamy brown, but now she looked darker, like her mother.

She couldn't tear herself away from looking at her own eyes. They were deep brown. Looking at them, she *saw* herself. But in them, she could see Eli and her parents, too.

CHAPTER 7

Naomi rubs her blue hands together, but the paint won't go away. She's straddling the seat of her Heliaride, the tips of her toes on the ground keeping her steady. Someone hollers her name. She rubs her hands against her pants, frowning at her stained fingers. She hears her name again, this time more demanding, so Naomi gives up on her hands and races to catch up to a group of kids. Some are her age, but most are older. They're all on Heliarides. She's almost caught up to them when the kid in front of her swerves by an old woman carrying a shopping bag. In one swoop, the kid snatches it out of the old woman's hands and flings the groceries across the street. Cans roll into the gutter. A bag of bread bursts open, followed by shrieks of laughter. The woman gasps and then curses. She glares at Naomi with her blue hands, as she coasts by on her bike. Naomi doesn't cower. With one hand on her handlebar, Naomi turns and smiles back, as if to say, What are *you* going to do about it?

Naomi opened her eyes, realizing that she had briefly fallen asleep on her back on the sidewalk in front of the smashed-up café. Her heart thumped in her chest as the nightmare faded, and Naomi realized where she was; not in camp, not with Lu and Shay, and not with her family. She bolted upright and called out for the coyote-dog, hoping it had come back.

Stiff and confused, Naomi stood up. She tried to recall exactly what the doctor had said. The memories would come in waves. They would be triggered by sights, sounds, or smells.

But he didn't say anything about nightmares. Even in camp, Naomi had nightmares. Dreams of being chased or looking at her hands and seeing that they had transformed into claws. The nightmare had felt like a memory, but that was the thing about powerful dreams. They felt real.

Her exhaustion had pulled her off course. She had fallen asleep on the sidewalk and ground her teeth through the nightmares. Naomi needed to get out of the canyon. Rest, as fitful as it had been, renewed her determination. She grabbed the backpack and walked swiftly away from the cafe toward the road that led into town.

On the way out of the shopping center, Naomi passed a board where people had once posted notices about missing pets or old furniture for sale.

Now, it was filled with faces—faces of missing people. Family members who had fled and not told anyone. Mothers who mysteriously didn't come home after going out for food rations. Fathers who were possibly arrested—or worse. There were dozens of notices, pinned on top of each other.

One notice caught her eye. One image of a girl with long black hair and deep brown eyes.

Naomi tore the notice off the board. *Missing*, the notice read. *We'll do anything to have her home.*

Naomi stared at the face.

It was her. According to the notice, she was missing and her family wanted her home.

CHAPTER 8

Naomi sat down on the curb and focused on the notice, willing memories to come back that would explain everything. Right now, nothing made sense.

In the Crisis Camp, the girls had been told that they were abandoned. Headquarters had made that very, *very* clear. The families could not take care of the girls, so they had turned them over to the Crisis Camp. It was a painful, yet responsible, action to take during difficult times. Headquarters had told the girls this over and over and over.

But the notice told another story. At some point, Naomi's family had been looking for her. Maybe they still were? If they had been looking for her, then maybe they didn't turn her over to the camp? Yet if that was true, how did she end up there?

Maybe something had happened to her parents? Had something happened to her?

Too many questions. Naomi slowly folded the notice and slid it in her pocket next to the ball.

The power is out in the neighborhood and across town. Mama wants them all to sleep in one room. Eli is in the big bed with Mama and Papa. Naomi is on a pile of blankets on the floor next to the bed, using a sheet for a blanket. Everyone except Eli is awake and silent. The house feels lopsided, off-balance, with all of the inhabitants in one room, sheltered, yet scared, while the rest of the house is empty and still, without even the buzz of the small refrigerator they used for milk and cheese. One of Headquarter's big trucks thunders down the street. Papa slips out of bed and goes to the window.

"They're arresting him next door," he whispers in a high voice. He almost sounds like a boy.

"Come back to bed," Mama says. "Come."

"I should do something," Papa says. "He's a friend. He'd do something for me, right?"

"What can you do?" Mama says, her voice rising. "There's nothing we can do."

"But—" Papa begins.

"Do you want to get arrested too?" Mama asks. "Do you want to leave us? There's nothing we can do."

Papa's shoulders slump. Naomi can't listen any longer. She puts the pillow over her head and squeezes her eyes shut.

Off-balance. That's how Naomi felt now with the folded notice in her pocket next to the ball. This message, desperately written by her parents, was in one pocket, on one side of her body. The rest of her felt tethered to it.

She stood up, balancing her weight on both feet. It was time to move on–for real. She had already spent too much time at Outpost #5. The questions would have to wait. She had to stick to her plan and get out of the canyon to town.

Naomi made her way back to the main road, empty and useless now that so many people had left the Canyon Region. She walked in the middle of it, following the yellow line.

Suddenly, she heard an old song Papa used to listen to. *In the night's light, in the day's darkness, you and me, baby. Save the light, save the darkness, you and me, baby.* But it wasn't soft and playful, like the version Papa would listen to. It was screechy and angry, as if the singer was making a joke of the song's sentimentality.

The song got louder. Naomi wasn't alone on the road. The disturbed version of the song was not playing in her mind. It was blaring from a solar music player attached to a junky Heliaride, spray-painted blue, ridden by an older boy who was barreling down the hill at her, a huge grin plastered to his face.

The boy skidded to a stop next to Naomi and tossed his bike to the side, the radio still howling. He grabbed her shoulders and playfully shook her. She ripped herself out of his grip, but he didn't seem to register her response.

"No way! Naomi! I forgot all about you. I mean, not really. But sort of. Wow! You got out? They let you out?"

The boy stepped toward her and Naomi took several steps back. She knew him, knew his face and his voice, but she couldn't remember who he was.

"Headquarters took my memory in the camp, but then I got it back," Naomi said slowly. She studied the boy's filthy face. Pimples spread across his forehead, which had a thick scar above his right eyebrow, and his lips were dry and cracked. His clothes looked stiff from days, or weeks, of dried sweat. He was skinny, too skinny, with wrist bones that stuck out like knobs.

"Naomi!" he howled her name again. "How wild! Out of the Crisis Camp. Got the memories back. Here, with me on the road." The boy stood his bike up, turned off the music player, and patted the handlebars.

"Get on! Let's go see everyone. Oh Naomi, you won't believe the place we've got now. You're going to freak out when you see it."

"Who are you?" Naomi asked.

The jumpiness in the boy's eyes settled and he tilted his head like a little kid, struck with curiosity.

"You don't know who I am?" he asked. "For real?"

"I know that I know you. I just can't remember everything—yet," she said.

For a second, Naomi detected hesitation in the boy's expression. It seemed like he was debating whether or not she could be trusted, like he might run, or turn to rage. But then his vulnerability vanished, and the boy licked his cracked lips. "Pooch," he said. "I'm Pooch."

Reflexively, she smiled. "Pooch?" she said slowly.

He rubbed his belly. "I am Pooch. 'Cause of my poochy belly! Well, it used to be poochy. But, you know. Not much food left anymore this high up in the canyon. We ate everything in the big house. Most of the other houses, too. Their owners left a long time ago. We're still trying to stay out of sight. Keeping away from Hirelings. Don't worry much about seeing too many other people up here in the canyon. Just a few ranchers left, living thin. And us."

Pooch paused his rattle, took a breath, and smacked his hand down on the handlebars. "Get on!" he demanded with a smile. "Let's go!"

He saw Naomi looking strangely at the Heliaride. "You like it? It's different right? We don't got power in the big house. So, we had to outfit our Heliarides. Turned them into old-fashioned bikes. Pedal to make the wheels go round and round. Manual power, you know?"

Pooch kicked the two flat pedals rigged to the bike frame. Then he gestured to the handlebars again. "What are you waiting for, Naomi? Let's hit it. Let's go see the boys."

Before Naomi could decide, Pooch's expression shifted. His mouth formed a tense line, and he grabbed her arm. "Hear that?" he said, biting down on his lips.

This time, she didn't pull her arm away. She listened, and yes, she did hear something, a low rumble in the distance, coming from up the road, the direction she had come from.

Pooch looked around spastically. "Over here!" he said, dragging his Heliaride behind a cluster of bushes.

Naomi stood still watching him as the sound grew louder. "Get over here!" Pooch said. "Hirelings! You want them to take you back to camp?"

Naomi's heart lifted. Camp? In that moment, the Crisis Camp seemed like exactly where she wanted to go, away from Pooch, who she couldn't remember, away from the painful memories that she had no control of, away from the nightmares and back into the tent with her friends, with Lu.

The crunching of tires against gravel grew louder. Pooch called out to her again. Naomi pressed her hand against her pocket. *We'll do anything to have her home.*

She sprinted toward the bushes, diving out of sight.

CHAPTER 9

In the dirt behind the bushes, Naomi had no choice but to press against Pooch, trying to make herself invisible from whoever was coming down the road. She could smell his skin and his rotten, hungry breath.

The brakes on the trucks squealed as the truck rounded the corner. Behind the bushes, out of sight, Pooch seemed more relaxed.

"Watch this," Pooch said, barely stifling a giggle.

He pulled a neon pink object from his pocket. Naomi stared at it. In camp, they had nothing so playfully bright and strange. Suddenly, the term came to her: water gun.

She reached across Pooch's lap and touched it with the tip of her fingers to trigger memories of undoing the cap, suctioning up water from a big blue bucket, feeling the heat of concrete sidewalk under her feet, enjoying cool water dripping down her arms. There had been one in the neighborhood, which all the kids shared.

"You want the honors?" he asked, offering her the gun. "Go for it."

She shook her head, confused. What was Pooch going to do?

A Hireling truck was in full view now, likely making its way from Camp, down the canyon, into town. Naomi tried to see who was driving, but the bush obscured her view. It occurred to her that the Director, or even the doctor, could be in the truck.

It drove by their hiding spot. "One, two, three," Pooch counted out loud to himself and then quickly shimmied on his stomach out from the safety of the bush.

He took aim and fired at the truck.

A stream of watery blue paint shot out of the gun. Most of it splattered across the dirt and the road, but some of it landed on the back of the truck.

Naomi stared at the blue streaks on the back of the Hirelings' dusty white truck. "Bingo!" Pooch said, shuffling back to Naomi. "What a shot!"

He smiled at her, waiting for praise, and reached out his hand for a high-five. Stunned, Naomi felt removed from her own body as her hand rose to slap Pooch's palm. Her compliance widened his grin, and Naomi found herself sucking in her lips in an effort to keep herself from smiling back. What was she doing?

Then the truck stopped, and the driver cut the engine.

"Oh no," Pooch said. "No, nope. Oh boy. What now?"

Naomi dug her fingernails into her palms, her eyes trained on the driver's door.

Pooch wouldn't shut up. "Do you think they saw? What do you think is going on? Let's run. You think we should run? We should go. They probably know we're here. We don't want to get caught."

"Shhhh," Naomi said instinctively. "Wait."

Quietly, she crouched on her heels next to Pooch, who couldn't quit fidgeting.

Suddenly, the truck engine roared back to life, and the Hirelings drove off.

"Free!" Pooch shouted, jumping up confidently, as if a moment before he hadn't been seized with panic.

Naomi stayed in a squat, waiting for her heartbeat to slow down. "Why did you do that?" she hissed. "With the paint?"

Pooch cocked his head again, looking at her strangely. "What do you mean?"

"What if they had seen?"

"We could have outrun them. Easy. No big deal. I got my Heliaride. And you're fast. You were always fast," Pooch said, righting his bike.

Naomi crossed her arms, steadying her breath.

"Man, they must have done a number to you in the camp. What happened? You don't seem like the old Naomi. You're all scared and serious and calm now. No offense, Naomi, but you seem like an old fart."

Pooch cracked up at his own joke.

"Everything in the camp was fine," Naomi muttered.

"Whatever," Pooch drawled. "What a weird thing to say. But hey, what do I know? Never went to a camp. Never gonna go. Not me. Not Pooch." He waved his hand across the handlebars.

"Let's get back to the house. Don't you want to see the boys? Don't you want to know what we've been doing? We'll tell you everything!"

Naomi *did* want to know. She wanted to know about why Pooch seemed to know her so well. She thought about how Shay and Lu said that she wondered too much, that it wasn't good for her. This was probably one of those times when she should clamp down on her wondering, get back to the task at hand, getting into town.

Yet, unaccustomed to making decisions, vulnerable to her own curiosity and confusion,

Naomi climbed onto Pooch's handlebars, and balanced herself in the middle.

It wasn't until they were off the main road, coasting down a bumpy driveway, speeding toward a mansion with a fake adobe façade and an ornate tiled doorway, that she remembered with a start the folded notice in her pocket and frantically pressed her hand to it, reassuring herself that it was still there next to the silver ball, and scolding herself for getting off course of the most important thing—finding her family. But then again, she was now with someone who knew her, someone who might have answers.

CHAPTER 10

Papers fly out of the classroom, like giant moths toward light. The door, removed from its hinges, lays flat in the middle of the dark playground, dozens of feet away from the room itself. Inside, in the science corner, plants have been ripped from their pots. The Beta fish are dead, floating at the top of their bowls. A desk, hammered with the heavy base of a microscope, one of the school's precious treasures, was used as a ladder to reach a top cabinet, where nuts had been kept, snacks for kids who had forgotten theirs. The cabinet has been gutted; nothing remains. There's a puddle of piss on the teacher's chair, and in the middle of that, a cracked framed photograph, a young teacher with a puppy in her lap, licking her cheek. Books and magazines smolder in a metal trash can, the pages charred and then doused in piss, too.

Naomi wanders around the room. A poster of a man in a large white suit, his face invisible behind the dark visor of a helmet, stands on the moon, next to a flag. At the whiteboard, she uncaps a pen, pauses. She feels an urge to write something but doesn't know what to write. A warm night breeze pushes through the broken windows and sends more papers out the door. Without writing anything, Naomi pockets the pen and leaves the classroom.

On the playground, there's laughing and screaming. Naomi gravitates toward the chaos. She feels like she's floating as she moves toward the swing set. No aim, no purpose. She's simply moving.

A boy sits at the base of the slide, his feet braced on the rubber mat in the sand below him. Lu is in his lap. The boy's arms are wrapped tightly around her. Lu silently strains against him, trying to get up. Purposely, he loosens his grip, goading her to escape. She tries to push up, away from him, and then he slams her back against him, grunting. They repeat the motions, over and over. Lu trying to get up and the boy forcing her back to him, jamming her into his lap. Neither speaks. Other kids run by chasing each other, unaffected by the boy and Lu.

But now Naomi is standing in front of them. She can clearly see what is happening, that the boy has imprisoned Lu in his arms. Naomi can see that Lu wants to be released.

Lu locks eyes with Naomi, while her body goes limp, and the boy squeezes her even tighter. Nobody says anything, but Lu's eyes speak to Naomi. Help me, they say. He's hurting me.

The boy squares his jaw, challenging Naomi to do something. Her eyes land on a fresh, angry scar that extends from the middle of his bottom lip to the tip of his pointy chin. What can she do? There's nothing she can do to help Lu. She could tell the boy to let Lu go, but he won't listen. She could make a fuss, but then what if he released Lu and grabbed Naomi, instead?

Naomi nods to the boy and shrugs to Lu. Naomi does nothing. She floats away.

Naomi quietly moaned as the waking nightmare faded. She was still on Pooch's handlebars, but now they were stopped at the end of a long driveway, in front of a salmon-colored mansion with a wide, wrap-around porch. Pooch tapped his foot, waiting for her to jump off. "Home sweet home," he said.

Naomi slid down, shaken. Inside of her, worry was building. The doctor had been so clear: the shot would restore her memories, and yet, this was the *second* vivid nightmare she'd had since she'd left camp.

A frightening thought struck her—what if the shot wasn't working? What if something had gone wrong? What if the nightmares continued to come on stronger and faster? Could the doctor fix it? Could he give her another shot? She wasn't supposed to return to the camp, but Naomi couldn't imagine enduring these waking nightmares for much longer. For the second time Naomi realized that she may have no choice but to head back up the canyon, from where she had come from, even if it meant begging to be let back in the camp, even if it meant any number of sacrifices, including finding her family.

For now, Naomi prayed that the nightmares would stop, and shakily she followed Pooch into the mansion.

It had been trashed. The stench of body odor and aging garbage greeted her at the door. Couch innards were spewed across the entryway. A gold-painted ceramic sculpture of a heron had been beheaded. Most of the windows were broken. Blue paint streaked down the cream-colored walls.

"Hey!" Pooch hollered. "Look who I found out on the road!"

Two boys appeared at the top of the second-floor landing on old-fashioned skateboards, narrow wooden boards with four plastic wheels, which they rode down a long, thick velvet rug that had been positioned on the stairs like a ramp to the first floor.

Unlike Pooch, the boys were not jumpy. Like Pooch, they were both filthy and skinny. They circled Naomi, confused. "You?" one asked.

"It's Naomi, dude," Pooch said, punching the boy in the upper arm. "They let her out of the camp.

She doesn't remember everything. But look? See? It's really her. I found her on the road. Heading toward town all by herself."

Pooch threw himself into an overstuffed chair covered with stains. "You remember these guys, right Naomi?"

Naomi stared at the boys. She remembered they were from school, a couple grades ahead of her. Rust was the tall one with greasy black hair.

The other boy was Glitch. She remembered a dusting of freckles across his nose, his wide stance, his pale, hollow eyes. But it was his scar that made her gasp. It cut down the center of his pointy chin, just like the boy in her nightmare squeezing her precious Lu.

CHAPTER 11

"What are you looking at?" Glitch barked, rubbing his chin.

Naomi averted her eyes, trying to shake the memory.

Pooch kicked off his battered shoes, sending them flying into a standing clock with a smashed face. "She's looking at your nasty scar, man. Remember the night you split your chin? Remember, Glitch? Hirelings chasing us. You running all crazy wild. And then—splat. You tripped on the curb, skidded across the street, chin first. Oh man! It might have been funny, if it wasn't so ugly. Right, Rust? That one Hireling, the fat one with the red cheeks, just inches from grabbing your ankles when Rust nailed him with that rock. Remember? Rust pelted him. Got him right in the helmet. Made a dent. Saw it with my own two eyes. Yep, and then you were back on your feet, zoom, bloody face, running down the street like a horse from a stable on fire. Remember?"

Glitch and Rust ignored Pooch.

"We don't got food," Rust said, crossing his arms. "Don't got anything to give you. Nothing to share."

Naomi nodded. "I don't need food. I'm not hungry."

Glitch snickered. "Not hungry?"

Rust eyed Naomi's backpack. "What's in there?" he asked and took a step toward her.

Naomi sensed that lying would lead to trouble. She slipped off the backpack and removed three food packets. She tossed one to each boy. Rust and Glitch tore theirs open with their teeth and devoured the food, sucking down the thick goo. Pooch ate his slowly, savoring each taste. "Mmmm," Pooch moaned. "So good. Yum."

After the boys ate, Pooch launched into a long, animated version of shooting the Hirelings' truck with the water gun full of blue paint.

"Then like a lizard, no, an iguana, no, a cobra, I slithered out on my belly. So stealthy. Smooth and quiet. I steadied the gun." Pooch dropped to the floor, reenacting the attack.

"Naomi was right behind me. 'Now,' she said. Perfect timing. Partner work. Perfect partners. Bam!

Pulled the trigger. Paint shot all over the back of the truck. Doused it. Blue streaks everywhere."

"Not exactly," Naomi muttered, but the other boys didn't acknowledge her, immune to Pooch's exaggeration.

Pooch continued, "And then, the truck screeched to a halt. We heard shouts, and—"

Naomi pressed her hand against her pocket with a surge of motivation.

"I'm not sure why I'm here. I've got to go," Naomi said.

"No, don't go," Pooch begged. "Stay."

Rust shrugged, uninterested in whether Naomi left. Glitch was lying on his back on the floor, staring at the ceiling. It didn't seem like he'd even heard the exchange.

"The Crisis Camp," Pooch said. "Tell us. We wanna know everything, all about it."

At the mention of the camp, Glitch sat up and faced Naomi.

"Yeah, tell us," he said. "Tell us about the camp. Why do you want to leave, anyway?"

"My family," Naomi said in a voice smaller than she intended.

All three of the boys laughed. "Your family don't want you—if they're even still in town," Glitch said.

"And they're probably not," Rust said. "Most everyone has left—or is leaving."

Naomi pressed her hand against her pocket where the notice was safely folded. She sat on the floor, leaning against the wall. Why did these boys seem to know her so well? They were Wilds, surely. But they acted like she had been a friend. She had so many questions. Not enough memories were emerging to make it clear.

With a sudden urgency, Naomi realized that she needed Pooch, Glitch, and Rust to fill in parts of her story. Without their information, she was going to carry on lost. She didn't like the boys and didn't trust them, but they could help her.

"I'll tell you about the camp," she said. "What do you want to know?"

"What'd you do there?" Rust asked, crossing his arms.

"Mostly, we worked. Picked fruit in the orchards, pruned the trees, weeded, fixed the irrigation lines. That sort of thing."

"How'd you know how to do it?" Pooch asked. "I mean, you hadn't done that kind of work before."

Naomi paused. The first few weeks she'd been at the camp were hazy in her memory. "I guess they taught us."

"Who?"

"The Hirelings? The Director?" Naomi suggested. "It's actually hard to remember. There just weren't that many adults around. It was mostly kids."

"What else did you do?" Rust asked.

"Work took up most of the day. But when we weren't working, there was a tent, a large one, where we went to talk or play card games. It's where we ate too. Some of the girls did the cooking, but not me. That wasn't one of my jobs," Naomi said.

"What'd you eat? How often?" Pooch asked, eyes widening.

Naomi described the flatbread, smeared with avocado from the orchard. She talked about the bitter coffee, fresh oranges, and broth made from the chickens they would slaughter weekly. She told about occasional glasses of goat milk and small tomatoes, the kind that tasted sweet like candy. As she spoke, she watched spittle form in the corner of Pooch's mouth.

"I'm so hungry," he said. "You don't even know."

"I don't believe you," Glitch hissed. "No way Headquarters fed you like that. Goat milk? Please."

"It's true," Naomi insisted, more afraid that Glitch would think she was lying than believe she had actually been well-fed. "We had two meals a day. They weren't big, and we never had meat. But we did eat."

"Liar," Rust said.

"No meat," Glitch scoffed.

"Look at me. Do I look like I've been starving?" Naomi said.

The boys rolled their eyes up and down Naomi's body, and instantly she was flooded with regret that she'd brought that kind of attention to herself. She pressed her arms against her chest and looked away.

"There were lectures," Naomi said, trying to change the subject. "They told us about the Crisis. How much trouble there was. How dangerous life was outside the camp."

Glitch chuckled. "Dangerous," he repeated.

"Where'd you sleep?" Rust asked.

"Tents," Naomi explained and paused, reluctant to mention Shay and Lu. "A lot of the time we did nothing. We laid in our tent and listened to the sounds of the orchard, girls giggling, wild turkeys squawking. At night, we heard coyotes. I could even hear the sea, or at least I thought I could."

For the next hour, the boys continued to ask question after question and Naomi answered them all. She told them about the boredom, the fog at night, the Director's announcement, the tired doctor with the syringe. Everything. She tried to describe what it had felt like to have no memories, no ideas or stories of life outside of the camp, except for those provided to her by the Director and the Hirelings.

"For example, I knew what school was," Naomi said. "The Director showed us pictures of school, kids sitting at desks, teachers writing on large boards. But I couldn't remember going to school or what types of things happened there. Also, the moon. I couldn't remember what it was. None of us could. We thought it might be a large star, but we didn't understand why it changed shape over time. Or rather, *I* wondered. I was curious about a lot of things that I knew I had once known but could no longer remember."

The boys listened attentively, like small children at story time, transfixed with the details of a place they had feared and avoided throughout the Crisis.

"Doesn't sound so bad," Pooch said eventually. "Food and games. Tents and friends."

"We did work," Naomi said. "A lot."

"They didn't hurt you?" Glitch asked.

"Nobody hurt us," she said. "Why would they?"

The boys looked at each other, disbelief coloring their grimy faces.

"Because you are Wild! Because every kid in the Crisis Camps is Wild! That's what the Crisis Camps are for. Keeping Wilds locked up," Pooch said. "It's jail, dummy."

Naomi scrunched her lips. It was her turn to look confused. "Not me. I'm not a Wild. That's not why I was there."

For once, Pooch was quiet. Rust shook his head in disbelief, while Glitch rolled his skateboard across the floor so that it smashed into the wall, making a huge dent in the plaster. "Yes, you, Naomi," he said. "Wild. Just like us."

CHAPTER 12

Half of her face is sandy. Crusty drool seeps out of her lips, and her mouth tastes sour. She's been sleeping on the beach. Over the ocean's horizon, the sun is poised to appear. Daybreak. She sees boots, many of them, kicking up sand. Hirelings are stomping around. A pile of blue Heliarides are nearby. Kids around her wake and try to run. In their sleepy state, the kids stumble, fall. The Hirelings tackle them, even the ones who are already on the ground. Naomi doesn't move. She doesn't try to run. The sand is cool on her one cheek. Finally, the sun rises completely over the horizon and suddenly the full force of daylight is in her eyes. So, she closes them, concentrating on the chilly sand on her cheek, not the sounds around her of kids crying and fighting back. She's so tired. She's ready to give up.

Naomi hugged her knees to her chest, trying to grasp the truth. The nightmare she had at Outpost #5 and the one she had on Pooch's handlebars were actually memories. Now, in the mansion, more resurfaced.

She had been like the boys. When the Crisis was at its worst, she had willingly left her family. She had abandoned Mama and Papa and Eli and had run away with the other Wilds in the Canyon Region. Not immediately, of course. At first, she rode her Heliaride around with a few of them when there was nothing to do, when the schools had been shuttered and their parents were distracted and worried.

But then it became more than kids loose and bored. It became a *thing*. Headquarters called them Wilds because they followed no rules. They had impulses and they acted on them. They stole groceries from older women and scattered them on the street. They broke the doors off the classrooms at the schools and pissed inside.

They had done so much worse.

Who was going to stop them?

This realization—that she wasn't who she thought she was—paralyzed Naomi. She sat stiffly with her back against the wall, rolling the ball in her pocket, while the boys climbed up the stairs and barreled down on their old skateboards, over and over and over. After a while, they seemed to forget she was there, leaning against the wall, trying to reconcile the truth of who she had actually been with who she had assumed she was.

The rhythmic sounds of their bodies and skateboards smashing against the ground, the grunting, the cursing, was like a heavy blanket, weighing her down, making her unable to move. How could she have turned away from her family—who were so good and scared and loved her so much? How could she have left them? Why had she done that? What was wrong with her?

More questions. No answers.

A flash of black fur streaked out of the kitchen, past Naomi's feet, and dove under the couch. A tail, gnawed raw, stuck out from underneath the couch. Naomi tapped her fingers against the floor, capturing the cat's attention. It stuck its head out from under the couch, revealing a pink nose and scabby bumps around her ears. "Here, kitty," Naomi whispered, catching Pooch's attention.

"That's Trouble," Pooch said. "Flea magnet. Super skittish. Don't even bother trying to pet her. She only likes me. I'm the only one she'll go to."

Naomi found that hard to believe, and yet the cat didn't budge from the cave-like safety of the couch. Naomi kept drumming her fingers on the floor. The cat's nose twitched, but she didn't move.

Naomi glanced up to the second-floor landing. Glitch had a vase in his hands.

"This is pretty," he said in a mock nice voice. Then he threw it over the banister and it shattered into hundreds of pieces on the floor, the crash sent Trouble out from under the couch, back towards the kitchen.

What was the purpose of the destruction? Naomi could recall a feeling, a temporary rush of excitement, when she broke something, when she hissed an insult in someone's direction, when she cackled like a feral animal in a roving pack of other uncontrolled beasts zooming around town on their Heliarides. But she also remembered that the teeny, tiny thrill was usually followed by a punch of regret, shame, and fear that made her queasy.

Now, she watched the boys in the mansion. It didn't seem like they were feeling anything anymore—neither the thrill nor the regret. They seemed numb, destroying things out of mindless habit. They had no purpose. It scared her.

Naomi stood up. "How did I get to the Crisis Camp?" she asked. "When did it happen?"

Glitch looked up at the sound of her voice, surprised that she was still in the mansion with them. He tucked his skateboard under his skinny arm and went out the front door, to the porch. Naomi followed him. It was dusk and a warm gust was shaking weak leaves off the branches of the oaks.

"You don't remember how you got to the camp?" he asked. She shook her head.

"We were on the beach a few months ago. Sleeping in the sand. A bunch of us. It had been a night with all sorts of wildness." At the memory, he smiled, baring his teeth.

"Hirelings showed up. We woke up and ran, but they got a lot of us, including you. That was the beginning of the end, as they say. Hirelings swept through town. Nabbed most of us. Threw everyone in the Crisis Camps. Some of us got away though—me, Rust, Pooch, some others. We came up into the Canyon. Not sure where the others went."

That nightmare was a memory too. Naomi had been on the beach when the Hirelings came. She hadn't tried to run. She was exhausted, so they took her, brought her to the Crisis Camp.

"The truth is," Glitch said. "Your family didn't leave you. *You left them.* Then you got caught."

Glitch stretched his skinny arms, holding his skateboard above his head. "We're free! We do whatever we want. Whenever we want. Life is good."

Naomi seethed with disgust. How could Glitch be proud of what he had done and who he was? He had nothing now. He was starving high up in the canyon, hiding from Hirelings, stuck in a wrecked mansion with two boys who could turn on each other at any moment.

"Hey, was Lu in the Crisis Camp with you? I always liked Lu. She's cute," he said. "Real cute."

Now, the disgust was a rotten taste in Naomi's mouth. She was nauseated by Glitch and furious with herself. How could she even be talking to the boy who had hurt someone she cared about so much?

Naomi's cheeks reddened with her feelings for Lu, and she felt the urge to punch Glitch, to take her fist and smash it into his nose, to send him spinning down the stairs of the porch onto his butt. Her anger was so acute. Why shouldn't she hit him? He deserved it. Didn't he?

Naomi dug her fingernails into her palm, creating a tight fist. She tried to summon Lu in her mind. What would Lu want her to do? She would want revenge, right?

Suddenly, Glitch stood up straighter and dropped his skateboard.

"Someone's coming," he said.

CHAPTER 13

The boys' senses were sharper than Naomi's. Like Pooch, Glitch could hear someone approaching before she did.

A girl with thick, messy blonde hair and a frown coasted down the driveway on a Heliaride, rolled to a stop, and regarded Glitch with the lift of her chin. The stiffness of Glitch's body loosened. Like the boys, she was thin and ashy. A bruise under her eye was a sickly green. She wore layers of clothes and boots, even though the day was warm. Unlike the boys, Naomi had no memory of the girl.

"Axe," Glitch said to the girl. "Been a few days."

"I was in town," Axe said. "Foraging."

"Find anything good?" Glitch asked.

The girl reached into her coat and pulled out a bag of mushy oranges.

"Nice," Glitch said and reached out his palm.

Axe grunted and handed an orange to Glitch. He peeled off the moldy skin.

The girl nodded and glared at Naomi. "Who are you?"

"Naomi," Glitch said, answering for her. "She just got out of the camp."

The girl raised her eyebrows with genuine surprise. "Really? Camp?"

Naomi nodded.

"They let her out," Glitch said. "Gave her memories back."

"Alright," she said and offered her an orange, soft with black spots.

Naomi cringed, but she accepted the offer, out of the girl's sweaty palm, the creases in her skin caked with dirt.

"Axe!" Pooch said, appearing on the porch. At the sight of the food, he and Rust rushed down the steps.

"Just one!" Axe snapped and swatted Rust as he tried to grab the oranges.

"What's going on in town?" Glitch asked.

"Exodus," Axe said. "Same story. Everyone is leaving."

"Leaving?" Naomi repeated, pressing her hand to her pocket.

"Naomi wants to find her family," Rust said, rolling his eyes.

Axe crossed her arms and took a step toward Naomi. "Wait a minute. Let me get this straight. You just got out of camp and you want to find your family. Why are you *here*?"

It was the exact question Naomi herself wanted to know, but before she could respond, before she could say that she had just come for answers, that she was trying to figure out who she had been, Axe's skinny fingers reached out and tugged on one of Naomi's backpack straps, causing her to stumble forward, toward the blonde girl.

"What's in your pack?" Axe demanded.

She looked at Glitch as she said it, seeming to blame him for not sorting this out already.

"They gave it to me when I left camp," Naomi said lamely, peeling Axe's fingers off the strap. "It's all I've got."

"*All I've got,*" Axe mimicked her. "What's in it?"

"Food packets," Rust said. "The goo kind. Sure she's got more."

"More," Axe spat. "Why aren't you sharing, Naomi? I shared my oranges with you."

Naomi lamely offered the moldy orange back to Axe. "Here. Just take it back."

"What?" Axe exploded. "You don't want my gift?"

Glitch nodded, as if he'd seen this scene before, as if it was unfolding just how he predicted it might, and Rust chuckled. In fact, they looked more alive than Naomi had seen them all day, giddy with the conflict erupting in front of them. Pooch started hopping from foot to foot.

"Nah, Naomi wants the orange," Pooch said. "Right, Naomi? You love oranges! Everyone loves oranges. Eat it. Come on, Naomi. It was a gift! Then you gotta give Axe a food packet. We all share. Gotta survive. Gotta do what's right. Lots of sharing in this big house."

"I don't want one food packet," Axe said tightly. "I want her pack. The whole thing. All the food packets and whatever else is in there. Give me your pack, Naomi."

Naomi sucked in her breath, while Pooch slipped back in the house. She thought about her pocket knife, the one she'd use in camp to slice open avocados or sever twine, the one they took from her when they left her on the road. She wished she had it now.

"Give me your pack," Axe repeated. "Or I'm going to take it—for keeps."

Naomi's options were limited. Glitch and Rust stood at attention, eager for excitement of any kind. Naomi didn't want them to defend her. She didn't want anything to do with them. But what other choices did she have? She gave them a pleading look, which they didn't even register. Naomi was on her own.

To get off the porch, Naomi would have to push past Axe, and while Naomi sensed that she was stronger and healthier than the girl, Axe's movements were too quick, refined over months of survival. The green bruise under Axe's eye told Naomi everything she needed to know about what would happen if she tried to muscle her way past her.

Resigned, Naomi began to slip one of the pack straps off her shoulder. Then Pooch shouted to them from the upstairs window. "Hey guys! Up here! Check out what I got!"

The four of them looked up to a second-story window. Naomi gasped. Pooch had Trouble by the tail and was swinging her from side to side, at least 20 feet in the air. Trouble snarled and tried to swat him, claws extended, but she was helpless in his grip.

Naomi felt like throwing up. "Don't!" she cried out.

Pooch met Naomi's eyes and for a moment, she felt something pass between them, a story behind a story, an inkling of Pooch's plan, but in a blink it was gone. Axe, seeing that Naomi was upset, cackled.

"Do it!" Axe called up to Pooch. "Hurl her out the window! Cats always land on their feet."

"They do?" Rust asked.

"Let's see," Glitch said. He licked his lips.

Naomi took a step away from them. "Ready to fly?" Pooch asked Trouble in a tinny voice.

"Fly! Fly! Fly!" Rust, Glitch, and Axe chanted in unison, pumping their fists in the air and pounding their feet on the ground. Naomi glanced over her shoulder at the pile of Heliarides, mere feet away.

"One!" Pooch swung Trouble to the left.

"Two!" He swung her to the right.

"Fly! Fly! Fly!"

Naomi did not wait for three. She ripped off her pack and threw it at the back of Axe's head.

"What the—" Axe swung around, jaw tight, ready to pounce. But then she saw the pack and dropped to her knees, ripping off the cord that kept it cinched at the top.

Glitch and Rust went down too, pulling out water, clothes, and food packets. Pooch yanked Trouble into the window and disappeared.

Naomi didn't hesitate. She stole a Heliaride from the pile on the ground and pushed on the rusty pedals as fast as she could, flying down the driveway, down the road, until the muscles in her legs burned.

CHAPTER 14

"Find something to do," Mama yells.

Naomi is frustrated, too. "Don't yell at me," she yells at Mama.

"Don't yell at me," Mama hisses back. "Please, Naomi, just find something to do. Papa and I need space to figure things out. You've got to get out of my hair. We're not working anymore. We don't know what's going to happen. We all might need to leave the Canyon Region. You know this is serious. Papa and I need to talk, privately."

Naomi steams. There is nothing to do. School is closed. She's stuck in her house everyday with her family. Everyone is worried and mad.

She gets her Heliaride out of the garage and heads out. She is allowed to go to the beach and back by herself. But she goes in the opposite direction, east through town, toward the canyon and the hills. A group of older kids from school are at the Healiaride ramp park. She sees them in the distance, down the main road.

She isn't allowed to go that far. But Mama told her to find something to do, right? She wants her out of her hair? She needs space to "figure things out," right? Naomi keeps riding.

Naomi was pedaling down a hill, in the dark, on the stolen Heliaride, picking up speed. As memories passed through her, she chewed her lip and kept pedaling.

Eli is sobbing. "Where were you?"

Naomi is at the sink, trying to scrub the blue paint off her hands. "You were gone for so long. Papa was so scared. He was crying."

"Hush," Naomi barks at Eli. He cries harder. There hasn't been soap in the house in over a week. The paint isn't coming off. She hears Papa stomping down the hallway. She braces herself for a fight. But there is no anger on his face, just relief. The skin around his eyes is red, swollen.

"Please, please," he begs Naomi. "You're only 11. It's so dangerous out there. You must stay here. Don't leave again." Naomi feels an urge to go into his arms, to cry, to confess, to apologize, to sink into him, and let it all out—but something stronger than that instinct has taken hold inside of her. Standing her ground, whatever that

means, seems easier than giving in to the fear and vulnerability of family.

"Whatever," she says under her breath and rolls her eyes.

On the stolen Heliaride, she had traveled far into the night, soaring down the main road. The boys and Axe seemed capable of just about anything. They were bored, angry, and hungry. She wondered if they would try to find her.

Naomi wanted to get far away from them, but where was she going? To town? How could she face her family now, knowing that she had caused them so much pain? How could she face them now that she wasn't even sure of who she was?

They are playing cards in the camp tent after working all day. Lu deals eight cards, instead of seven. She's made this mistake before. It's no big deal, but it makes Naomi laugh. Lu simply can't remember the rules of the game. They've told her so many times. When she laughs, Lu lashes out, kicking up the mat where the cards are laid out. Other girls look up. Lu doesn't have outbursts. Hardly anyone has outbursts in the camp. Then, she begins to cry. Lu's emotions paralyze Naomi, but Shay knows what to do. She wraps her arms around Lu and mumbles reassuring things in her ear.

"I don't know why I did that," Lu says. She's trying to calm down, but still, she gives Naomi an untrusting

look. It makes Naomi's cheeks burn. All she did was laugh. No big deal, right? But it seems like there's more to it than that, for her and for Lu. The whole episode is over in minutes. Lu deals the cards correctly, Naomi smiles as they play the game, and Shay peels an orange. Friends again. Everything is fine.

Miles from the mansion, Naomi began to slow down. She felt ill. Glitch had wrapped his disgusting arms around Lu, pinned her to him, and Naomi had done nothing. She hadn't been brave enough to stand up for her friend. In the camp, with no memories, some part of Lu must have known this. The feeling must have still been in her even if she couldn't remember why. Naomi had cared about Lu, and she had cared about her family. Why had she acted the opposite way of how she felt?

The moon had been providing enough light for Naomi to follow the yellow line in the center of the road. But now, fog was crawling up the canyon, blocking the light of the stars and the moon.

Naomi knew she was going down, down was the only way out of the canyon, but it didn't feel that way. The darkness was disorienting. Now that she wasn't pedaling as fast, her sweat started to dry and a coolness settled on her skin. She yearned for the jacket rolled up at the bottom of the pack she had thrown at Axe's head. She yearned for the sleeping bag in her cot, near the warmth of her friends. She yearned for her bed, in her family's home, her home.

Lost in these desires, Naomi didn't see the large brittle branch in the road. Even if she had been focused and warm, she likely would have missed it. The darkness was so complete.

The front tire of her bike jammed against the branch. Unexpecting, Naomi didn't even brake. The bike tipped forward and to the side, and Naomi flew off. The left side of her body smacked the pavement, and the bike crashed down on top of her.

Naomi moaned, trapped under the back rusty wheel, which was still spinning on top of her. She used her right arm to push the bike off and rolled on to her back. Her left hip and elbow screamed with pain. She ran her right fingers along her elbow, smearing wetness down her arm. Even without being able to see, she knew it was blood oozing from a deep wound.

The road still held the day's heat, and despite her misery, the warmth felt good. Naomi wanted to sleep on the road, to escape the pain in her body and the agony in her mind, but she pushed herself to her feet.

Steadying herself, she took a step into the darkness. Pain radiated from her left hip, sending ripples of hurt both down her leg and up into her back. Gasping, she dropped back down to the road again.

Naomi began to bawl in disbelief and anger. How could she have been so stupid? Why was she trying to ride in the dark? What did she think was going to happen?

Crying only caused more pain. The tears brought on a headache that had already been building from hunger and thirst and fear.

Naomi forced herself to stop and to rise to her feet again. Wincing through the pain, she hobbled to the bike and stood it upright. Both the handlebars and the rim of the front tire were bent, and that tire wouldn't spin. It was worthless.

Naomi released the bike back onto the ground and limped off the road to lean against a tree. Behind her, she could make out the outline of rows of trees, likely an abandoned orchard. It smelled like camp, and that smell brought back peaceful memories, of lying under the trees after a day of work, of joking with Shay, of knowing nothing, *nothing*, of the horrible, cowardly person she had once been.

Her family had not abandoned her; she had abandoned them.

Exhaustion became a heavy weight, overpowering the pain in her hip and arm. She sunk down into the weeds at the base of the tree. Was she going to sleep on the ground? She thought of the predators who roamed the canyon—black bears, mountain lions. They probably wouldn't be a threat.

But what other threats were there? She realized that the Director had said the Crisis was over, they were on the other side of it, but what did that mean? Hirelings were still around, traveling the road, going from town to camp and back again. Axe had said that people were leaving town, but not everyone. Who was left?

Naomi wanted to scream with the regret she felt about leaving the camp. What had she been thinking? Shay was right. She and Lu were like Naomi's family. She had been safe with them even if Lu didn't trust Naomi completely, and even if Naomi was restless. In the Crisis Camp, she had friendship and avocados smeared on flatbread and goat milk and card games and peace. What a gift it had been to remove her memory! A merciful thing, which she didn't deserve.

But then there had been the pull. The word she heard in her mind. *Come.* The awareness of something outside of the camp, down the canyon, that she was connected to. The familiar pleasure she felt when she rolled the ball between her thumb and index finger. Had she stayed, none of that would have gone away. Her curiosity would have grown. She was sure of it.

From nearby, a coyote howled. What if Glitter had been tracking Naomi through the night? "Glitter?" she whispered and waited, straining to hear if the animal was approaching.

Again, a coyote howled. This time, it seemed farther away.

Naomi cradled her left arm across her stomach and tried to find a position that didn't aggravate the pain in her hip. She rested her head on the back of the tree and let herself close her eyes, allowing the weight of the day push her towards sleep.

But then something ripped her awake. Laughter. Through the darkness, someone was coming down the road.

CHAPTER 15

Their voices were distinct, even though Naomi couldn't make out the words. Glitch and Axe were coming down the canyon.

Naomi heard their low chatter and the whirring sound of their bike tires against the gravel. As quietly as she could, she dragged herself behind a cluster of trees. Underneath her body, dead leaves broke and split, making a deafening sound that she was sure would give her away. She tried to remind herself of the dozens of other creatures—raccoons, foxes, opossums—roaming the canyon, crunching leaves in the chaparral. She hoped that Glitch and Axe would think that the sounds were coming from an unthreatening animal.

Dim lights bounced along the road. Glitch and Axe had solar-powered lights attached to their bikes. With lights, they wouldn't crash into the branch and worse, they would see her bike. If they saw her bike, they would find her. With Naomi's injuries, there was no way she could outrun them.

Soon they rounded a corner, and as Naomi predicted, they stopped in the road, in front of the branch.

Glitch kicked Naomi's bike. "Mangled. Somebody ate it," he said. "Bad crash."

"Wait," Axe said. "Isn't that Pooch's bike? The one Naomi took?"

"Nah," Glitch said. "His bike is bigger."

"You sure?"

"Yeah, I'm sure. Also, there's no way she made it this far in the dark with no lights," Glitch said.

"Well, whose bike do you think it is?" Axe said.

"I don't know!" Glitch sounded annoyed. "You know there's still freaks running around this canyon. Could be anybody's bike."

"Whatever, Glitch," Axe said. "I actually don't care who's bike it is. We gotta get that train. Let's go."

Naomi squeezed her eyes shut, willing Glitch and Axe to start moving again, but Glitch didn't move.

"You sure we shouldn't be taking Pooch and Rust? You sure we should have left them behind?"

"Oh come on, Glitch. They'd slow us down. We've gotta get out of *here*. Trust me. There's nothing worth anything in this canyon. Town is trash. And I'm done running from Hirelings."

"Yeah. But Pooch and Rust are going to have a hard time on their own."

"I. Don't. Care."

Glitch still wasn't moving. "Where we gonna go, anyway? Hirelings are everywhere."

"Wherever the train is going! People are leaving. We need to leave too."

"*People* aren't us. *People* can get on a train."

Axe sighed. "You know what? You sound scared. Are you scared, Glitch? I don't want to be doing this with anyone who's scared. Maybe you need to go back to that stupid mansion with your ridiculous friends."

Glitch kicked the wheel of Axe's bike. "I don't know what you're talking about. Nonsense talk. I'm not scared of anything."

"You're totally freaked out, Glitch!" Axe teased. "Like you've never hopped a stupid train before."

"Pooch and Rust will starve here," he said. "They just don't—"

"I don't care about them!," Axe said. "Do you? Really? I care about getting out of here. Full stop." She started riding away, curving around the branch.

"Coming?" she called back.

Glitch spit on the road. Then he got on his bike and road off into the darkness behind Axe. They kept talking, but their voices didn't carry. Naomi could no longer hear them.

Slow tears of relief spilled down Naomi's cheeks as she allowed herself to breathe again. Glitch and Axe were no longer a threat, even though Pooch and Rust still could be. For now, she just had to worry about her banged-up body and the striking truth that the Canyon Region was emptying out and any chance of finding her family, if that even made sense anymore, was becoming increasingly out of reach.

CHAPTER 16

Early night was giving away to deep night. Fog had penetrated this high area of the canyon, carrying a familiar, moist, salty sea scent. Naomi shuddered, feeling her way through the darkness slowly, mindful that the ground was a minefield of stumps and ditches. She didn't want to fall again, but she figured this was her best bet for the night. Away from the road and deeper into the neglected orchard. She just wanted to find a soft patch to lay down and rest on until the sun rose and she could carefully assess her injuries and come up with a plan.

Then, in the darkness, Naomi heard singing. At first, she thought it was in her mind. In her exhausted and confused state, the melody was too tender and sorrowful to be real. Before her grandfather died, he had prayed on Friday nights. The memory of her grandfather lighting candles and praying, waving his hands gently in front of his face as if to beckon the light, surfaced. When Naomi visited him, she prayed too, even though she wasn't sure why. She didn't know what the words meant. They were in another language. But she hummed along with her grandfather. She stood next to him and allowed the flames to warm her face.

Naomi crunched through the dead leaves, stumbling over exposed roots, following the singing, humming along to a familiar prayer that surely she was just hearing in her mind. How could someone actually be here singing, high up in the canyon, in this abandoned orchard? Then she saw it: lights flickering in an open cottage window. The wind teased the candles but the flames burned strong. A woman prayed, like her grandfather had.

The orchard wasn't completely neglected after all. Naomi recalled what the boys had said. The woman was likely one of the few people who had stayed in the canyon.

From inside the cottage, dogs began to growl, sensing Naomi outside. The woman's prayers were interrupted. "Something out there?"

The woman spoke to the dogs, and Naomi tasted the bitterness of panic for a second time. If the woman opened the door to let the dogs investigate, not only would she be found, she would be hurt.

Ranchers trained their dogs to protect their property—at any cost. Those dogs were probably the reason why the boys and Axe hadn't trampled all around the ranch themselves.

Running would be too noisy—and it seemed nearly impossible. Naomi's hip thumped with pain, which coursed up and down her left leg. Staying still was her only option. She squatted to the ground and dropped her head. Invisibility was unachievable, but stillness she could accomplish. She had done it before, near the road when she hid from Glitch and Axe.

She inhaled deeply and slowly, letting the air seep out from between her lips. Her fingertips rested lightly on the ground, ready to launch if she needed to break into a sprint, as painful as it might be.

The snarls ceased. Now the dogs were barking, but it wasn't an alarmed bark. It sounded like they were just chatting it out. "Hush," Naomi heard the woman say. "Quiet now."

There was a weak whimper and a whine, and then the dogs quieted. Naomi's adrenaline faded and exhaustion overwhelmed her. She waited until the woman retreated deeper into the cottage before she quietly crawled to the window and sat beneath it. It wasn't safe on the woman's ranch. But it wasn't safe anywhere. The night had made that clear.

The sounds of the woman shuffling around her home were the last Naomi heard before she fell asleep.

CHAPTER 17

A siren blares and everyone rushes to get into their homes. Strong salty wind whips off the ocean, blowing sand through the streets of town. Eli trips on a crack in the sidewalk and howls in pain. Naomi scoops him into her arms and runs into the house. Safely inside, she studies the ripped skin on his knee. The band-aids are gone. The medicine is gone. She blows on the cut to ease the sting. Eli buries his face in her hair and cries. She holds him. Mama and Papa are out, trying to find food. The kids will come around soon. They will call to her from the street on their Heliarides, beckoning her to come ride with them.

Naomi awoke on her right side, her back against the wall of the cottage, a bed of dry leaves beneath her. Her face and hands were cold. She had fallen asleep under the praying woman's window. Now it was daylight and the woman and her dogs were going to discover her if she didn't go quickly.

She rubbed the sleep from her eyes and focused first on what was on top of her: a quilt with faded patches in warm shades of orange, brown, and pink. Then she honed in on the thing on the ground next to her: a turquoise tray with a black and white diamond pattern. On the tray was a peach mug with steaming minty tea. There was also a plate with fluffy scrambled eggs and thin slices of persimmon.

The sight was too much for Naomi. The beauty of it enflamed a brief, bewildered rage in her. She didn't deserve this breakfast. Did she?

But the sharp, demanding hunger quelled her guilt, and she fed herself, quickly, without a second thought. When the food was gone, she picked up the mug and blew on the steam. The minty scent was good, so good. She brought the mug to her face and let the steam wash over her skin.

Then she set to examining herself. She couldn't twist her left arm at the right angle to see the wound on her elbow, but she could feel with her fingers that the blood had already started to clot and form a scab. Her stiff left leg ached as she stretched it out. She rolled down the waistband of her pants enough to see that a large, violet bruise was forming on her hip and the area was swollen, nearly double the size of the same area on her right hip.

Carefully, Naomi got to her feet, steadying herself before picking up the beautiful tray to bring to the front door of the cottage. It was open. Inside were dozens of lines of drying persimmons, strung from the rafters. The furniture was old and worn, but it was a clean, cared for home.

"Come in?"

Naomi spun around.

The praying woman was behind her, flanked by three dogs, holding a basket of linens. "So sorry," she said. "Didn't mean to startle you. I was just pulling in the sheets from the line with my pups."

The dogs wagged at the sound of their owner's calm voice and one gently nudged Naomi with his snout.

The woman was tall, with wide hips and a narrow torso. Her tan skin was covered in taupe freckles across her face and down her arms. She wore ranch clothes: faded, thick pants, rubber boots, an oversized buttoned shirt, rolled up to the elbows. Her rose-colored hair had wide streaks of gray and was piled into a nest on the top of her head. She set down the basket of linens.

"I recognize you," Naomi said. "You sell persimmons at the market on Sunday. Sometimes you are there with another woman."

"Hanako, my wife. We used to sell at the market, before the Crisis."

Naomi handed the woman the tray. "Thank you," she said.

"Was it tasty?" the woman asked.

Naomi nodded. She wanted to say more. It was *so* tasty. It was the best thing to happen to her since she had left the Crisis Camp. She felt overcome with gratitude, but the words wouldn't come.

Tears came instead without warning or sound. They slid down her cheeks, down her neck, under the collar of her shirt. Naomi felt like she was melting from the inside out, from the warm tea and food and peace of the praying, persimmon woman's land, where she'd spent the second half of last night, alone but safe.

The woman held the tray with one hand and placed her other hand on the back of Naomi's right arm—it was a gesture Naomi immediately remembered that Mama used to do—and guided her inside her home, toward a rickety kitchen table steadied by a wadded rag under one leg, where Naomi sat embarrassed at her own inability to speak, as the woman brewed more hot water to make more minty tea.

CHAPTER 18

In the kitchen painted in sunlight, the woman talked and gathered supplies while Naomi listened and sipped her fresh cup of tea. Her tears had stopped flowing. But still, she couldn't speak. She looked for signs of Hanako, but it seemed like the woman lived alone now.

"I've been on this land since I was a little girl. Got a well. Chickens, when the foxes and coyotes don't outsmart me. Persimmons, of course, and some avocados too. Plus, my own vegetable garden. I can't run the orchard anymore. No help. But I have enough. My dogs keep me safe. They're well-trained. Don't need much more than that. But other ranchers—"

The woman's voice trailed off. She had introduced herself as Joslyn. Naomi had told Joslyn her name and that she'd had a Heliaride accident but not much else. Joslyn hadn't asked questions. A huge mutt with thick ivory fur and a tail full of burs slept under the table at Joslyn's feet. Occasionally, he would shift, and Naomi would feel him knock against her legs. The two other dogs, each small with black and white markings and pointy ears, slept in a heap on the couch.

Joslyn pulled a chair close to Naomi. "Let's see what's going on here," she said.

Naomi raised her arm so Joslyn could see her elbow. She poured a few drops of solution from an unmarked bottle into a rag and dabbed Naomi's arm, first gently, and then she began to scrub. When Naomi bit her lip, Joslyn didn't apologize, but she explained, "Got to get the gravel out of here. Could cause an infection."

Fresh blood began to flow from the wound. The scent awakened the mutt, and he shifted out from under the table. The other dogs awoke, too, and one gave a short yip before falling back asleep. Joslyn took a clean rag and wrapped it tightly around the wound. Then she examined Naomi's swollen hip. She pulled a glass jar from a cabinet by the sink, unscrewed the lid, and handed it to Naomi, who spread the soothing gel around the bruised area.

Joslyn moved quietly around her house, returning the items she had used to tend to Naomi.

Squatting by the cabinet under the sink, Joslyn startled Naomi with a question.

"Do you know what caused the Crisis?" Naomi realized that even though she had been living through it, she didn't know the answer.

Joslyn answered her own question. "Greed. Plain and simple. Headquarters, those selfish crooks, made bad decisions for a long time. Decisions to make themselves rich. Always about getting more and more. Always thinking about now. Never concerned about the future or the people, who suffered. Our people. But there's only so much people will take before they rise up. That's the story again and again, throughout history, throughout time, all around the planet. The rich can treat the people like dirt—to a point. There's always a point when the people rise up."

The mutt shifted, and Naomi reached under the table to scratch his head.

"In my experience, people basically want two things: to work and to take care of their families. People want to feel productive. They want to feel like they are getting something done. So when the jobs demand too much and pay too little, what happens? Well, in the Canyon Region, some people left. They got passes to go to other Regions. But the other people? Stuck. Nowhere else to go. I am too attached to this place to leave. My family had this land before Headquarters took over the Canyon

Region, before there even were Regions. Way back when there were fewer borders, when people moved without permission from Headquarters, when representatives elected by the people governed, not Headquarters."

"When Headquarters made things too hard, people began to fight back," Naomi said, surprising herself at her own contribution to the conversation. She rolled the ball in her pocket.

Joslyn paused, studying Naomi's face, waiting for her to continue.

"One night, my neighbor got arrested for fighting back," Naomi said. "Papa watched from the bedroom window as Hirelings took him away. Papa was scared. I could tell. He wanted to do something, but Mama wouldn't let him."

Joslyn nodded. "Did your parents protest? Did they fight?"

Naomi shook her head. "They were taking care of me and my brother."

Joslyn nodded again, approvingly. "Headquarters responded to the people's anger by taking more things away, infuriating people even more. Closed the schools. Shut off the power. Raised prices on food even more. This went on for a while, right? The tension was building. And then things got chaotic. People turned on each other. People went wild and did stupid things. That was a horrible time. You know."

Naomi stared at Joslyn. She studied Joslyn's soft green eyes, flecked with brown. Did Joslyn know about Naomi? Did she know who Naomi was and what she had done?

Joslyn rose from the table. She turned her back to Naomi while she sliced a persimmon into thin, half-moons. Naomi looked around the cottage, trying to find something to distract her, to settle her thoughts.

"Go ahead. Walk around," Joslyn said, sensing Naomi's curiosity. Naomi stood up and stretched her back, stiff from the accident and the night on the ground.

On the wall next to the pantry were bookshelves. Most of the books looked very old, in thick faded paper covers. They seemed to be about things related to the land and food, with titles like *Seeds for Every Season* and *The Art and Science of Pickling*. The top shelf, though, was full of thin books with worn spines.

"Hanako liked poetry," Joslyn said. "That's part of her collection."

"Where is she?" Naomi asked and then regretted the question.

Joslyn paused; her knife raised slightly above the fruit. "She died last year."

"I'm sorry," Naomi said softly. Immediately she began to see signs of Hanako's absence and Joslyn's loneliness. On the mantle above the fireplace, there was a picture of Hanako, sketched with brown charcoal. Around the picture were dried thistles and seeds and a few shells.

"She drew that picture of herself," Joslyn said. "I can't do those things. Draw. Understand poetry. But I've been trying more, since she died." After Joslyn had arranged the persimmon slices on the wooden cutting board, she sat back down and folded her hands in front of her. Naomi sat down again, too. She ate several of the slices, as Joslyn gathered things into a bag.

"Do you think you can walk a bit?" Joslyn asked.

"I'll try," Naomi said and winced.

"Nah," Joslyn said. "You need to rest to heal. We'll take my Heliaride. I try to conserve the energy, but I haven't used it in a while, and we don't have far to go."

"Where are we going?" Naomi asked.

"Out for a bit," Joslyn said without elaborating and grabbed a canvas bag from a hook on the wall.

Unlike the boys' Heliarides, Joslyn's still ran on power. It was also outfitted for the ranch, with thick-treaded tires and a small wagon on the back, which Naomi rode in.

The dogs jogged along as Joslyn navigated a flat, rocky trail that led through the orchard to an overgrown meadow, where Naomi spotted their final destination, a small cottage, smaller than

Joslyn's, in the shade of a massive, sprawling oak tree. As they got closer, Joslyn pointed out the remnants of rope swing in the tree.

"Spent hours playing on that when I was a little girl," she said.

After parking the bike, Joslyn wordlessly marched into the meadow and pulled flowers, red fuchsia, white yarrow, and a stalk of indian paintbrush. She took a rusty can out from her bag and arranged the flowers in it. Naomi followed Joslyn into the cottage.

The front door hung from one hinge, and both front windows had been smashed. Inside, mold streaked down what tattered strips of the patterned wallpaper were left. Mice droppings crushed underfoot as they went into the main room, where sunlight shone through a hole in the roof.

The only object in the room was a collapsed metal bed. Without ritual, Joslyn set the can of fresh flowers next to it and removed a can of wilting, dead flowers.

"My favorite uncle," Joslyn said as she straddled the bike. "Kind of a cranky, judgmental guy with most folks. Always quick to tell people what they were doing wrong. But he loved me. One summer he broke his leg and I brought him flowers every day. Cheered him up, for a second. He was the last of my family members to leave the Canyon Region. I still bring flowers. Just once a week, now."

"Where did he go?" Naomi asked.

Joslyn shrugged. "Doesn't really matter, does it? Once people leave, we usually don't see them again. It was that way before the Crisis too."

Naomi followed Joslyn back outside. "Hunter!" Joslyn bellowed, startling Naomi.

"More than anyone in the world, including me, my uncle loved Hunter," Joslyn said. She whistled, waited, and then whistled again.

"Broke his heart that he couldn't take Hunter with him," Joslyn explained. "The animal is fine on its own. But I still bring him some meat, if I have it."

She whistled again, pulling a few pieces of chicken skin out of her bag. The dogs rushed to her feet. "Stop begging. You know this isn't for you. There he is," Josyln said, nodding toward a creature who emerged from a eucalyptus grove at the far edge of the meadow. Her dogs began to growl, but Joslyn hushed them.

"Glitter!" Naomi shouted.

Now it was Joslyn's turn to be startled. "What in the world are you talking about?"

"That coyote-dog followed me around a bit yesterday," Naomi explained carefully, leaving out details. "I called it Glitter."

Joslyn chuckled. "His coat is thick as a board. He's got scabs up and down his backside. And he's missing a chunk of his tail. Why in the world did you call him Glitter?"

Naomi paused, unsure whether to share her memory of Mama. But Joslyn went on.

"Anyways, I think you have the wrong dog. This one is scared of absolutely everyone but my uncle. He won't even come up to me, and I have chicken skin. I have to toss it, like this." Joslyn threw the skin into the tall grass, and the coyote-dog sprinted to grab it, before slinking back into the shadow of the grove.

"No, he let me pet him. He was by my side for a bit," Naomi insisted. "Watch."

Joslyn raised her eyebrows and crossed her arms.

"Glitter! Come here, boy," Naomi called to the dog. From a distance, she could see him wagging his tail.

"Glitter! Come on," Naomi called again. She walked away from the house, toward the grove, feeling Joslyn's eyes on her. The dogs began to follow Naomi, but Joslyn called them back. Naomi squatted, beckoning to the coyote-dog. He inched towards her, his head lowered. When he was a few feet away, Naomi reached out her hand. He sniffed her fingertips, before jogging off, back into the shade of the eucalyptus.

Joslyn wore a disbelieving smile on her face. "Okay, Naomi," she said. "Okay."

She started the Heliaride, clicking for her dogs to come along. Naomi felt a surge of pride, having won Josalyn's approval. But as they rode away, she looked over her shoulder at the cottage. On the outside wall was a faded blue "W." Naomi gasped, but Joslyn appeared not to hear.

Whatever Joslyn thought of Naomi now, Naomi knew it would all change when the ranch woman learned the truth.

CHAPTER 19

Back at Joslyn's, Naomi rested her head on her arm on the table.

"I'm sorry, Joslyn," she said softly. "I'm so tired. I can't even keep my head up."

Joslyn nodded. "Come with me."

Naomi followed Joslyn through the kitchen to a small room behind the pantry. Inside was a cot covered with the hand stitched quilt Naomi had woken up under that morning. Naomi didn't wait for permission. She removed her shoes and slid into the cool pocket between the quilt and the sun-dried sheet, asleep before Joslyn slid the threadbare yellow curtain along the rod, barely filtering the late-morning sunlight.

Mama cracks an egg into the pan. Butter splatters and the rich smell makes Naomi's mouth water. She hoovers behind Mama, watching the egg cook, the golden yolk tightening in the pan. The door opens, and Papa comes in, scowling.

"Eggs? Butter? Where did you get eggs?" With each word, he raises his voice more.

Mama turns her back to him. "You know where. I don't know why you're asking."

"Why would you take that risk?" Papa slaps his hand on the counter, making Naomi jump.

"Stop it," Mama growls. "The children need food. Real food. Not pouches. I don't care if it's right or wrong. I'll go again. Anything I need to do to get them food, I'll do it. Don't even try to get in my way."

Papa shakes his head and runs his hand through his hair. His jaw is trembling, and it seems like he's going to shout. But then he leaves the room, and Mama uses a spatula to pull the fried egg from the pan, onto a plate.

Pounding. The distinct sound of fist on wood. Barking.

Naomi kicked off the quilt, breathing heavily, drenched in sweat.

More pounding. The faraway sound of Joslyn's voice, hushing the barking dogs.

Naomi wiped the sweat from her face, jammed her feet inside her boots, not bothering with the laces, and stood up tenderly. Somehow, it was already dusk, the blush sky darkening.

"Who's there?" Joslyn's voice was sharp, demanding. One of the dogs growled.

Was it Glitch and Axe? Had they missed the train and come looking for her? Or could it be Pooch and Rust? Had they come across the bike and followed her tracks to Joslyn's house? Images from the destroyed mansion flashed through Naomi's mind. Would they do the same thing to Joslyn's beautiful cottage? The dogs would protect Joslyn and her home, right? But at what cost?

Naomi hurried out from the room, dragging her left leg, just as Joslyn was opening the front door.

A Hireling marched into the cottage. He wore the plain uniform of the other Hirelings, but he wasn't wearing his cap. His greasy hair was messy, and he ran his fingers through it absentmindedly before regarding Joslyn with a nod.

"Mick," Joslyn said sternly as the Hireling noticed Naomi, raising his eyebrows slightly with surprise. Naomi took a step back.

Joslyn ignored Naomi. "You're two days early," Joslyn said. "You can't just show up whenever you want."

The Hireling shrugged. "But actually, I can."

Joslyn shook her head, her cheeks flushed with anger.

"Do you have it?"

"Of course I do, Mick," Joslyn said. "I keep my word." She stomped into the kitchen, opened the door under the sink, and pulled out a bag.

"Three pounds," Joslyn said. "Now go on and leave me alone. Next time, don't come early. Come when you're supposed to."

The Hireling stood his ground. "You can't talk to me like that, Joslyn."

Joslyn mimicked his tone. *"But actually, I can."*

The Hireling frowned. "Joslyn, if you report me, I will report you. We will both be in trouble. Big trouble."

Joslyn sighed. "Yeah, except one of us has a lot more to lose. Don't forget, I already lost what mattered to me. You, on the other hand, still have your family. Let's not play around. Stick to the deal. Don't come early."

The Hireling's shoulders rolled forward in reluctant agreement. He turned to go, but then looked Naomi's way. She tried to keep herself steady, to meet his eyes.

"Joslyn, we caught two Wilds sneaking onto the train last night," he said. "A boy and a girl. Mad as rabid bats. Skinny, filthy, and crazy. Shipped them off to camp." Mick looked at Naomi.

"Why are you telling me?" Joslyn challenged him.

"Just saying, Wilds are still up in the Canyon. We keep thinking we've caught them all, but they're slippery. You know? Smart, too. Schemers. Like rats. Difficult to catch."

Joslyn nodded and grinned. "Children can be very resourceful."

The Hireling clucked his tongue, not agreeing with Joslyn's snark. He crossed his arms.

"Still can't believe you let those punks squat at your uncle's place," Mick said.

"What else was I going to do with it?" Joslyn shot back. "It's not like I need two places to live. I didn't bother them, so they didn't bother me. It's really none of your business."

Mick rolled his eyes. "Who's *this* girl?"

"I'm Naomi." Naomi crossed her arms, too, to keep them from shaking.

Joslyn fidgeted. "*She* is also none of your business. *She* is my guest."

Mick cocked his head. "Your guest? Okay. Whatever you say, Joslyn. Where are you visiting from, Joslyn's Guest?"

"You don't have to answer, Naomi," Joslyn said swiftly.

Naomi didn't understand the relationship between Joslyn and the Hireling, but she felt clear about one thing. She wasn't going to lie or do anything to make life more difficult for Joslyn, who had provided her with shelter and so much kindness.

"I was in the camp. I chose to get my memory back. On the road, making my way into town, I had a bike accident. Joslyn took me in and helped me."

Joslyn's eyes widened, and Naomi couldn't tell why—whether it was approval from the directness in her tone, shock from the realization that Naomi had been in the camp, or fear about how the Hireling might respond.

He nodded. "Ah. You're the one. They told me one of the girls opted for her memory. So, how do you like it? Being here on the outside, with all your memories of your previous, beautiful life?"

He laughed at his own joke and didn't wait for a response. "I'll see you in two weeks," he grumbled to Joslyn and left.

Joslyn locked the door behind him.

CHAPTER 20

For a moment, Joslyn and Naomi were silent. Then Joslyn pulled on a flannel.

"Let's take a short walk," Joslyn said. "Come."

Joslyn said the word, the one word that Naomi had heard inside her own mind all those days in the Crisis Camp—*come*. Joslyn said it with authority, the way Naomi had heard it with certainty. So, even though Naomi was shaky from the encounter with the Hireling, even though questions bombarded her mind, she felt compelled to follow her.

She limped behind Joslyn, out the back door of the cottage, past the raised garden beds, through a tunnel of vines, around a small reservoir pond, to a wild, mammoth butterfly bush, more like a tree. Dozens of swollen cones of small purple flowers buzzed with life, as butterflies and bees flitted from one to the next, retrieving nectar. Joslyn slipped under the leaves and sat in the wide circle of shade cast by the towering bush, pulling her knees to her chest. Naomi joined her.

"This was Hanako's favorite plant on the property. Butterfly bushes are common around here, but this one is so unusual. We didn't do anything special to make it grow like this. It just seemed in charge of its own destiny," Joslyn said, adjusting the band that held her hair. "It's where I buried her ashes."

Naomi looked at Joslyn's face, heavy with grief. Why was Joslyn sharing this place with her? It wasn't what Naomi expected when Joslyn had beckoned her. Naomi wanted to know about the Hireling, why he was at the house, what arrangement he had with Joslyn. She wanted to know what Joslyn had thought about her admission that she had come from a Crisis Camp, and everything that admission implied about who she was and what she had done.

"When Hanako fell sick, we needed medicine and care. But as you know, that was hard to come by. At the time, my uncle was gone, but we still had friends living up here in the canyon with us. Old friends. Friends I'd had since childhood. They were preparing to leave and begged us to come with them. The other regions had medicine, supposedly. They had the medical services that Hanako needed.

Other regions were safer." Joslyn ran her hand along the thick trunks of the bush.

"I refused to go. I refused to believe that Hanako was *that* sick. But mostly, mostly, I didn't want to leave my land. This is *my* home. I couldn't imagine being anywhere else. Of course, I also couldn't imagine life without my wife. Hanko agreed to stay with me. Our friends were devastated—and mad. They thought we were stupid, foolish. They told us that we were being crazy. They left and their departure created a hole in our lives."

Joslyn paused and sighed. "Hanako got sicker and sicker. By then, it was too late to leave the region. We were stuck. I tried to take care of her on my own, but it was beyond me. There was so much I didn't know how to do. She was in pain, and there was very little I could do about it. That Hireling, the one who came today, knew my situation. Mick has a big family, and Headquarters doesn't even give the Hirelings enough. We struck a deal. I'd give him food I was growing here on the ranch, and he would smuggle me medicine. We said that we'd do it for a year, whatever happened. Then, Hanako died. The medicine wasn't enough to save her. And now I still owe that thug food."

Joslyn stuffed her hands in her pockets. "We should have left when we had the chance, but then, of course, we would have lost all this."

Joslyn spread open her arms, gesturing at the land around her.

"It's hard to know what the other regions are like. The way the land has thrived here, in spite of everything, I just don't think that's the case everywhere. We don't know cities. We don't know places where the land is parched or filthy. We just don't know anything but the Canyon Region, don't we?"

At a loss for what to say, Naomi apologized. "I'm sorry, Joslyn."

By then, the sun had completely disappeared, and the first stars were appearing. In the distance, the foghorn began to blow, a sign that night was on its way.

Naomi, Joslyn, and the dogs made their way back inside the cottage, where Joslyn boiled water for tea and lit candles. She quickly prepared eggs and sliced the bread she took from a tin bread box on the counter.

Joslyn had said her piece, and now it was Naomi's turn. She'd shared so little about herself since she arrived at Joslyn's, but it was time for her silence to end.

"Tell me, Naomi. Why were you sleeping outside my cottage last night?" Joslyn asked.

Naomi thought about when she chose not to fall into the embrace of her family, not to turn to them, not to lean into them, not to confess, not to be sorry—and she knew that choice had been a mistake. She wasn't going to make it again.

She gave into the urge to tell Joslyn her story, her whole story, and Joslyn, in her warm kitchen, sipped her tea and listened. As she spoke, hope began to burn in Naomi. Joslyn had taken Naomi in, treated her wounds, defended her to the Hireling, shared her own pain with her. She was alone on this beautiful, broken ranch. What if Naomi could help Joslyn as much as she had helped Naomi? An idea began to form, a way to save Naomi from facing herself and her past. She held this idea inside of her, deciding that she would wait to see how Joslyn responded to her story before she shared it with her.

When Naomi was done talking, cold night air blew in through the windows and the candles shivered. Joslyn had listened, but she hadn't spoken. Naomi had threaded all the painful pieces together as honestly and accurately as she could, and now it was Joslyn's turn to respond, to give Naomi her reflections, her thoughts. But she didn't.

"I'm tired, Naomi," Joslyn said, pushing her chair away from the table.

Naomi opened her mouth, stunned. Was Joslyn not going to share her reaction? Something about it felt unfair, or at the very least, lopsided. All of Naomi's stories seemed to hang in the air, unable to land. But Joslyn didn't explain herself or even give Naomi the promise that they would talk more tomorrow. She made her way to the bedroom with the dogs close at her heels, leaving Naomi at the kitchen table, staring at the tea leaves in the bottom of her cup.

CHAPTER 21

Papa hands Naomi a gift wrapped in red paper.

"Happy birthday," Mama says. Naomi tries to overlook that the gift is wrapped in the paper from the box of dry goods that is delivered once a week, not the shiny paper Mama used last year. She opens the present.

"The Night Sky," Naomi reads the title. It is a book she's borrowed dozens of times from the library, when the library had still been open.

"My own copy?" Naomi asks, bewildered at how her parents could have bought a copy when even socks were so hard to come by. She flips to page 89, a very old photograph of Earth taken from the moon, her favorite page.

Mama winces. "Well, not exactly. It's my friend's copy. She said you can look at it for a bit."

"A long-term loan," Papa says with a strained smile. "We'll eventually have to return it, whenever things start opening up again. Sorry, Naomi. It's not a good year for birthday presents, for anyone. It's the best we can do."

"Yeah," Naomi says flatly, running her hand along the cover, a picture of a telescope.

Papa had told her once that when his grandfather was a kid, it was common for people to actually own these instruments, which allowed them to see the details of the craters of the moon. Naomi still can't imagine living in a time when regular people could own something so powerful, so rare. A part of Naomi has always harbored a hope that Papa would uncover her grandfather's telescope in a box of old family mementos, forgotten all these years, although she knew perfectly well that everything of value had been sold long ago.

"Thanks for the present," Naomi says.

The next morning, when Naomi emerged from the small bedroom by the pantry, Joslyn gave her a thermos of tea, easing Naomi's suspicion that Joslyn was punishing her with silence. "I needed time to think," Joslyn said, explaining her abrupt departure from the kitchen table

Naomi could accept this. She, too, had a lot to think over, particularly the idea that she had been mulling over and was almost ready to propose to Joslyn. "How is your leg?" Joslyn asked.

Naomi stretched it out in front of her. "Much better. The swelling has gone down."

"Good. And your elbow?"

Gingerly, Naomi unwrapped the dressing, revealing a large scab. Joslyn nodded with approval. "You're ready," she said.

"For what?" Naomi asked, but Joslyn didn't respond. She walked swiftly out of the house, whistling for the dogs. Naomi followed them through the orchard to the edge of a dry creek bed. The dogs stuck close, stopping occasionally to pounce on a lizard or bark at a squirrel running along a branch overhead.

"In the winter, during a good year, this creek is swollen. Sometimes it even jumps its banks," Joslyn said. "It winds its way down the canyon, to the ocean, by town. It won't be wet for several months."

With steady strides, Joslyn hiked up the dry, silver creek bed, and Naomi followed, scrambling over exposed boulders that had been worn smooth over the years by rapid winter waters and through craters of gray and blue pebbles. Soon, they reached a steep vertical bank, which they climbed up. At the top was a flat rock that extended partly over the edge. They climbed to the rock and sat.

"In the winter, there's a waterfall here. Water rushes over this ledge. It's so loud, having a conversation is impossible—unless you want to scream," Joslyn said.

Now, the silence screamed. Naomi had told Joslyn her story, and still Joslyn had given no response. She had taken her to the rock, to a silent, invisible waterfall. She hadn't said anything about Naomi's confession. Her non-response was beginning to make Naomi uneasy again.

"So, you were a Wild?" Joslyn asked, although Naomi had already made it clear that yes, she had roamed with the others, the older kids, causing harm and destruction. She'd made it clear that she was caught and thrown into the camp.

"What was the worst thing you did?" Joslyn asked. "The thing that haunts you the most."

At the blunt question, Naomi squeezed her eyes shut. She searched for the right, honest answer. "I can't remember everything. The memories are still coming back. But I think the worst thing wasn't actually what I *did*. It was what I *didn't* do. Glitch was hurting Lu, I mean really hurting her. He was humiliating her, scaring her, and I didn't stop him. I didn't intervene. I acted like everything was fine and normal, when I knew it wasn't. I acted like I cared about nothing, like I was beyond caring, even though I did care about her. I still do."

Joslyn nodded. "A painful memory."

Naomi shuddered again. Joslyn placed her calloused hands on Naomi's shoulders and turned Naomi to face her. Naomi felt an urge to run, to dart into the woods.

Why had Joslyn led her to this place? Joslyn hadn't interfered when some Wilds stayed in her uncle's cottage. Naomi had clearly heard Joslyn defend the decision to Mick. But what if there was more to it? Joslyn had been so kind, so giving. She had given Naomi no reason not to trust her. So why was Naomi overcome with doubts?

Naomi forced herself to meet Joslyn's soft green eyes. It wasn't disapproval she saw, but reassurance.

"You are a child! You were an even younger child when you did the things that are tearing you up. You broke windows. Stole things. You didn't stand up for your friend. You caused your family pain. But you are not a bad person. Children cannot be bad people. You know that, don't you?"

A red-tailed hawk's shadow passed over them and they both involuntarily turned their faces toward the sky. The hawk soared on and Joslyn continued.

"Children, like adults, can make bad choices. Sure. You were responding to a world that was completely coming undone. It was easier to try and forget the pain and uncertainty by joining the chaos, rather than by resisting it. I get that. I really do. Often the right choice is the hard choice, the *really* hard choice."

In the Crisis Camp, without her memories, Naomi had thought of herself as a good person, a strong and steady person who worked hard and cared for her friends. But then she left the camp, the memories invaded, and she realized that she must have been wrong about herself.

"If Wilds weren't as big of a problem as they actually say, then why did Headquarters round them—us—up? Why did they take us away from our families? They took us away because we were making too much trouble. Because we were making everything worse."

Tears of rage clouded Joslyn's eyes. She inhaled sharply. "Naomi, listen to me. Supposedly, the Crisis is over. Some people have gone back to work. Hospitals are opening again. Schools may open soon. But still, people are leaving! Why is it 'over'? Why are things starting to get back to 'normal'? Is it because the people have gotten what they wanted? Absolutely not! It's over because Headquarters was finally able to subdue the people. They were able to get the people to back down and quit asking for the things they deserved to have—better wages, better working conditions, better food. How do you think Headquarters did it? How do you think Headquarters got the people to stop fighting, bow their heads, and give in?"

The afternoon was warm and dry, but Naomi was shivering like it was the dead of night, on a windswept, winter beach. She suspected that she knew the answer to Joslyn's question. But she didn't want to say it aloud. It hurt too much.

"Headquarters quelled the people by taking away the children. Headquarters took away the children, called them Wilds, embellished their minor offenses, locked them away in Crisis Camps, and stole their memories. Without their children, the people were beaten down. The people worried Headquarters would take more children—or worse. They gave in."

"I don't understand," Naomi said. "If all that is true, then why did Headquarters offer to give us our memories back?"

Joslyn snapped her fingers. "To beat the people down even more! To say, 'We gave your children the choice to get their memories and come home, but they didn't want it!' Headquarters knew that after all the lies they had fed you in the Crisis Camps, all the brainwashing, the children would not want their memories. They wouldn't want to remember their families abandoning them, which, of course, was never true."

"Headquarters was right. The children didn't want their memories back," Naomi said.

"Most of them," Joslyn said. "But one of them took her memories back. One of them reclaimed herself. One of them was curious and brave enough to face the unknown. Her will to know her true self was stronger than her fear not to."

"Me," Naomi whispered.

"Yes," Joslyn said. "You."

CHAPTER 22

"What if dogs could speak?" Eli asked.

"They do speak," Naomi said.

"I mean human-speak!" Eli said, wiggling his loose tooth with his tongue.

"What if the moon disappeared?" Naomi asked.

"What if we found a million dollars in the toilet?" Eli said.

"What if you grew an eleventh finger?"

"Good one," Eli said.

"Thank you," Naomi said.

"What if I changed my name to Zeli?"

"What if I changed my name to Zaomi?"

"What if I could pop out this tooth with my tongue?

"You can. Do it. It's been loose forever."

"Can I use my fingers?"

"Sure," Naomi said.

Eli stretched open his mouth, pinched his loose baby tooth, and shook it.

"Blood!" he shouted, delighted to see pink streaks in the spit on his hand.

"Keep wiggling!" Naomi said. "Get it out!"

"Gahhh!" Eli dislodged the tooth completely.

"You did it," Naomi said, squeezing him. "One less baby tooth for you."

"What if the tooth fairy forgets to come tonight?" Eli asked.

"What if."

Naomi laid back on the smooth rock, letting the warm sun temporarily blind her. Her hand drifted to her pocket. She was allowing everything Joslyn had said to sink in.

"You keep patting your pocket," Joslyn said. "What do you have in there?"

Naomi pulled out the folded paper and passed it to Joslyn. "I found it on a board in Outpost #5."

She sat up and watched Joslyn read it. "When do you think your parents wrote this?" Joslyn asked.

"I don't know," Naomi said. "It could have been when I ran away. Or it could have been when I got thrown into the Crisis Camp—before Headquarters told everyone they had taken the children."

Joslyn pursed her lips together, agreeing. "Your poor parents must be heartbroken. Naomi, it's time to go find them."

"I don't think I want to," Naomi said softly, ready to speak the idea she had been forming in her mind. "I want to stay with you. I could help you on the ranch. In the camp, I learned a lot. I work hard. I'm used to working from dawn to dusk. You wouldn't be alone."

"Why *wouldn't* you want to find your family? They're out there. They were looking for you."

"Joslyn, what if they haven't forgiven me? What if they have already left?"

Joslyn sighed. "Well, I don't know your family. I guess that's a possibility. But there's only one way to know."

Naomi tried not to cry. The thought of continuing her search was so daunting, and overwhelmed her heart. Staying here with Joslyn felt like peace, the kind of peace she missed from the Crisis Camp.

"There's something more important than finding them and getting their forgiveness," Joslyn said. "You must forgive yourself."

Naomi shook her head. "How could I ever?"

"How could you not?"

"What about you?" Naomi said, hot tears finally springing from her eyes. "Yesterday, you said it was your fault that you didn't leave the Canyon Region with Hanako when you had the chance."

Joslyn cocked her head to one side, studying Naomi. "That's not exactly what I said."

Naomi hugged her knees to her chest. She closed her eyes and recalled their conversation underneath the butterfly bush. "You said that you should have left when you could."

"Yes, but that's different," Joslyn said. "I don't blame myself for not leaving. I know Hanako didn't blame me either. We were faced with no good choices. Staying was wrong. Leaving was wrong."

Naomi took the ball out of her pocket and held it up in the sunlight. "I've got this too. A small silver ball. I found it in the camp, in the dirt. As soon as I found it, things began to change for me. It seemed so familiar to me but I didn't know why. I still don't. But the familiarity of it triggered a sort of opening in my mind. I felt…an awareness. It made me feel connected to the world outside the camp. I still can't remember what it's called."

Joslyn took the ball from Naomi and held it in her palm. "It's a marble. A child's toy."

"Marble." Naomi repeated the word.

She took back the marble and the notice and returned them to her pocket.

"This creek bed leads to the ocean? All the way into town?" Naomi asked.

Joslyn nodded.

"Yes, that's why I took you here. You can follow this all the way and avoid Hirelings that may be on the road close to town, though I doubt they'd give you any trouble at this point. I'd take you into town myself but powering up my Heliaride costs too much for the trip."

Naomi hesitated. "I don't want to go alone. Maybe I should go find Glitter and coax him into coming with me."

Joslyn shook her head and took off her backpack. "You can do this, Naomi."

"A thermos of tea. A container of water. Boiled eggs and fruit. A blanket if you need to spend another night outside. A clean rag for your wound. If you walk swiftly,yet carefully, you should make it before dark. I put a book in there, too. In case you need to give your mind a break."

Naomi leaned into Joslyn, and the older woman sighed, a sound Naomi remembered her mother making when Naomi was a little girl and would climb into bed with her in the morning, nuzzling her face into her mother's messy hair.

"I have so much to thank you for. You—," Naomi began, but Joslyn interrupted her.

"Please. You don't need to say anything."

Joslyn stood up and dusted off the back of her pants. "There's one more important thing I need to tell you. You probably heard me praying the night you arrived. Do you know what I pray for? The strength to do the right thing, *despite* our circumstances. You made mistakes and you're going to make more. That's okay. But when you do, get yourself back on the right course."

Naomi pressed her hand against her pocket.

"Maybe, one day, if Headquarters opens the market again, I'll see you there," Joslyn said. Then, before Naomi could respond, before she could express any more doubts or gratitude, Joslyn strode off the rock with her dogs, away from the creek bed, toward her home.

Alone on the rock, Naomi gazed west. Like the tide, sweeping away top layers of sand, Naomi felt pulled down the creek bed, out of the canyon.

CHAPTER 23

Papa's beard tickles Naomi's ear as he coaxes her awake. He whispers to get up quietly, to not speak, to follow him. The sky is still dark when Naomi peels open her eyes and wordlessly allows Papa to help her slip into shorts and sandals. He takes her hand and leads her out of their house, where they leave behind Eli and Mama, who is softly snoring.

It's not quite dawn, and the chilly air snaps Naomi awake. She treads behind Papa's long strides down the empty sidewalk to the beach, where the sea is an undisturbed dark sheet. A splintery fence separates the open sand from Trip's property. Papa picks up Naomi and sets her on the top horizontal plank.

"Jump into his yard," Papa says. "Then undo the latch on the gate and let me in."

Trip is Papa's friend, but since he scolded her for going into his tool shed at a party, Naomi regards him with wariness.

"Trip's not home. He's gone," Papa says. "Not coming back."

Naomi looks down at Trip's yard, full of his junk, a rusty shovel, a few tires, some dry paint cans.

There's no reason to whisper, but Naomi does anyway. "He left his stuff behind?"

Papa nods but offers no explanation. "Yeah, most of it."

"It's a high jump," Naomi says.

"You can do it," Papa says. "I've seen you jump from tree branches twice as high."

A surge of pride compels Naomi to leap, and she lands on her feet. Even though Papa said Trip isn't home, she still expects him to swing open the patio door and bark at her for hopping into his yard. Her hand trembles slightly as she undoes the gate latch.

Papa comes into the yard and pauses for a moment, looking around. He shakes his head slightly and mumbles, "Can't believe this."

Naomi's not sure exactly what it is he can't believe, but her parents have been muttering various versions of disbelief lately. Papa removes an old tarp, revealing Trip's scratched-up canoe, which he and Papa used to take out fishing. Papa grabs the handle in the front, and Naomi takes the one in the back. The oars are inside. The boat is lighter than Naomi imagines, and they easily guide it out of the gate, down the slope, to the water's edge.

The sky is still flecked with stars, and the horizon is a pale coral ribbon. Papa and Naomi kick off their sandals and toss them into the boat. Naomi gets in first, and Papa guides the boat into the sea, the water rising to his thighs. Then he clambers in and begins to row, away from the shore. Naomi peers over the side, dragging her hand through the cool, crow-black water.

The sky brightens as the sun's head pushes above the horizon. The stars above begin to disappear, and the water lightens, revealing the kelp just below the surface. Papa paddles and paddles and paddles until Trip's home is a doll house on the shore.

Naomi watches Papa row with even movements, appearing as strong and calm as she's ever seen him, despite the tears rolling down his cheeks. "Papa," Naomi says, and though she knows the boat will rock, she slips off her bow seat to get closer to him.

He sets down the oar and nestles his lips in her hair, kissing her head, while he cries into it. Rarely has she seen either of her parents cry and it startles Naomi, but she tries not to let it show.

Soon Papa wipes his face and points to the shore. In the intense daybreak light, the Canyon Region glows. The small coastal cottages with their salt-worn pastel paint look grand, but the hills, which rise up from above the town, look royal, unbeatable and blessed.

"Your home," Papa says. "We have so much, Naomi. So much to lose."

Even as the day heated up, Naomi didn't rest. Her hip still ached, but she trekked through the pain, drinking and eating as she went. Once she tripped over a sharp rock and sliced her knee through her pants. She cursed herself for being clumsy and wasting the time and water it took to clean the wound and get back on her path.

Her thoughts moved fluidly as she walked. No thought stayed long enough for her to get stuck on it. Her body moved and her thoughts and feelings moved with it.

After a couple of hours, a train horn broke her trance. Naomi stopped. How had she not noticed? Her concentration had blinded her. Rock, branch, root. Groove, lizard, rivet. She hadn't looked behind her, or even ahead. Now, she realized what she had missed. Train tracks ran parallel to the creek bed at this part of the journey.

Several dozen cows spread out across the tracks, grazing on the weeds that grew around the rails. Their ears were clipped with tags, but that didn't mean they were owned. They could be roaming on their own now. Whether wild or not, they weren't budging from the tracks.

A train rounded the corner, and immediately began to slow down, detecting the living obstacles in the way. Screeching, it came to a stop. The horn blared, but the cows were unaffected. Heads down, they continued to rip out weeds, chewing them with their square jaws.

Nearest to Naomi was a passenger car. A young child pressed her face to the window. She waved at Naomi with two fingers, and Naomi raised her hand while scanning the other windows, those in which the tinted paper had been peeled off, and she saw tired, somber faces. Some looked in her direction, but most stared straight ahead, lost in thought.

Naomi took a deep breath. The train was a distraction. She had to keep moving. The train was going away from town, and she was going toward it. Again, she began to walk, chin to her chest, down the creek bed, alongside the stopped train, passing two other passenger cars, and then cargo cars, with open doors.

"Hey!" someone hissed at her from one of the open cargo doors. Naomi shook her head, kept her eyes trained on her feet, indicating that she didn't want to talk. Rock, branch, root. Groove, lizard, rivet.

"Hey!"

Naomi watched her shoes, covered in dust. Her pace quickened.

"Naomi!"

A skinny boy lurked in the shadow of the open cargo doors.

Pooch.

CHAPTER 24

Pooch gestured wildly. "Over here! Naomi! It's me!"

When she didn't move from the creek bed, Pooch emerged from the shadows of the cargo car. He peered down the tracks at the train workers, preoccupied with the cows, and then jumped out, landing on his feet in the gravel. He leapt over a cluster of young manzanita bushes and made his way to Naomi.

"Wow! Destiny, huh? We meet again! Crazy. Naomi, out here by the train tracks. What happened to your elbow? All bandaged up. Where've you been? Where are you going?"

Naomi clenched her jaw, unsure of how to respond, bewildered by the sight of Pooch, jumping around in front of her, with his non-stop yabbering.

"Yeah, I know what you're thinking. The cat! You're mad about Trouble. Cute, filthy, dumb, flea basket. You didn't actually think I was gonna hurt her, right? Look, I'll tell you all about it. Axe is okay. She's alright. But she's got a short temper. Goes from zero to ten. Kind of like an animal herself. All instinct. All emotion. She doesn't really trust people, doesn't even like people. You know, especially new people. With you, I could tell she was getting a little, well, fired up. She was about to pop. Explode in your face. I was trying to help you. You know that, right? Hanging Trouble out the window? That was a distraction. I wasn't going to hurt that dumb cat."

Naomi softened. "Yeah, I guess I knew you were trying to help me. I kind of thought that."

Pooch grinned, revealing his stained teeth. "Good! That's right. You get it."

"Where's Rust?" Naomi asked, looking over Pooch's shoulder at the train car. "Is he in there?"

"Nah," Pooch kicked a pebble on the ground. "Rust wanted to stay up in the Canyon, but uh, not me. I was ready for a little adventure. Something different. Time to get moving."

He rubbed his hands together. "Glitch and Axe took off the night you left. I figured they went for the train. It's all Axe could talk about. Kind of bummed they left me with Rust. He's so grumpy. So lazy. But whatever. I'm gonna find them."

Naomi shook her head. "Axe and Glitch got busted, Pooch," she explained. "Hirelings caught them. They didn't make it out of town."

Pooch's mouth dropped open, but for once, he was silent.

"Glitch and Axe were thrown in camp," Naomi went on. "That's where they are now."

"How do you know?" Pooch asked.

"I just do. I heard someone talking about it."

"Who?" Pooch pressed.

Naomi shrugged her shoulders and rolled the marble in her pocket.

The train whistled. All but one of the cows had been ushered off the tracks, into the dry grass.

"The train's going to leave soon," Naomi said. "You should get back on before a Hireling sees you. You don't want to get thrown in camp too."

Pooch stuffed his hands in his pockets. "Come with me," he said quietly. "Come."

At the sound of the word, Naomi faltered and rocked slightly back on her heels.

"I don't want to be alone," Pooch said even quieter. "Do you?"

"I don't," Naomi said and meant it. "But I'm looking for my family, Pooch."

He chewed his lip, hopped from foot to foot. "Naomi, look, I know things were crazy. But I'm not bad. Not a bad guy. Not a bad friend. It's just been so—"

Naomi rested her hand on Pooch's shoulder, and with her touch, he settled for a moment into stillness.

Naomi didn't know what Pooch was like before the Crisis, but she had her suspicions—an energetic kid who loved being around people and making them laugh, someone who loved pranks and surprises, loved telling outrageous stories, and loved big uncontrolled parties. She wondered about his family and realized that he likely wondered about them too, but shame kept him on his own, kept him from trying to find them.

What Joslyn was trying to explain to her earlier started to make sense. Making bad choices in a world of bad options was understandable, even easy. If Joslyn had forgiven herself for staying on the ranch, even though it likely cost Hanako her life, Naomi could forgive herself for leaving her family. She could do the hard thing, which was also the right thing. She could get herself back on course.

Naomi couldn't give Pooch what he wanted, a friend, a traveling companion, but she could give him a part of what Joslyn had given her.

"I know you're not a bad guy, Pooch. We all messed up. It's a messed-up time."

The train whistled again, and the engine roared to life.

Pooch dug the toe of his shoe into the dust. "You're probably doing the right thing," he said. "Trying to find your family."

"Yeah," Naomi said.

"But Naomi, what if they're not there?" Pooch asked. "What if they've already left? What if they're on this train right here, behind me?"

It was a serious question that chilled Naomi, but it also made her smile.

"What if the train hits a cow?" she asked.

Pooch smiled back.

"What if a cow hits the train?" he asked.

"What if you swallow a bee while you're yapping?"

"What if you get bit by a rattlesnake while you're walking?

"What if you find a big chocolate cake, like the biggest chocolate cake ever?" Naomi asked.

"What if you lose your pants?" Pooch hollered and then slammed his hand over his mouth, remembering to not draw attention to them.

"Lots of what ifs," Naomi said. "Always."

The train began to move. Pooch gave Naomi a light punch in the arm and ran to the tracks. Naomi watched as he grabbed the low rung on a car's ladder, hoisting himself up just as the train picked up speed.

She expected Pooch to turn back and flash her a grin, but he disappeared into the shadows of the cargo car.

Naomi put her head down and resumed her journey down the dry creek bed, toward town and the ocean. Suddenly, the train screeched to a stop–again, and yet again, Naomi froze, scanning the landscape. But now there were no cows on the tracks, nothing out of the ordinary except small clouds of dust kicked up by a couple of Hirelings, running alongside the train toward Pooch's car.

CHAPTER 25

Naomi hit the ground and tried to suppress a cough as she breathed in dirt through her mouth and nose. From the ground, she couldn't see the train, but she could hear the sounds of a scuffle. Someone barking an order, a scream, a grunt, a smack.

She began to pant, unable to suppress panic, unable to achieve stillness. Thorns from a ground vine dug into her legs, and she twisted to get into a better position.

The sounds of the fight died down, but then she heard a command, loud and clear, from a voice that was undeniably Pooch's. "Naomi, run!"

Instead of running, Naomi began to crawl, inching her way forward in the dirt, trying to both stay hidden and get to some sort of vantage point where she could see what was happening. She hadn't traveled for more than twenty seconds when she heard the crackling of small branches being torn and broken. Someone was coming through the bushes, toward her.

The memory of the beach washed over her. She remembered the feeling of defeat, of giving into the cool sand, of kids desperately and heedlessly trying to escape, while she did nothing, allowing herself to be caught, to be taken from the fake safety of her feral friends. This time was different. She was alone, tired but awake, and she wasn't going to give up.

With a deep breath, Naomi rose to her feet, coming face-to-face with two Hirelings and Pooch. One Hireling gripped Pooch's skinny upper arm. Pooch's lower left jaw was swelling up. His captor's cheeks had fresh scratches oozing blood. The collar of his uniform was ripped, revealing part of a tattoo across his collarbone, a black arrow with a red tip.

"Aw, Naomi. I gave him everything I had. Fought like a cat. Like a wild, hungry feline. I tried to warn you. Didn't you hear–?"

The Hireling holding Pooch kicked his ankle, and Pooch whimpered.

"Take her," the Hireling grunted to his partner. "Get that Wild and let's go."

The other Hireling paused. Naomi met his eyes, tired and familiar, and sucked in her breath. It was the Hireling from Joslyn's house. His eyes flashed with recognition of her, and for a second, Naomi detected fear. He crossed his arms and stared at his boots, trying to regain his composure.

"I'm not a Wild," Naomi said.

She repeated what she had told the Hireling at Joslyn's.

"I was in the camp. I chose to take my memory back with the Memory Restoration Act. I'm making my way into town, back to my family."

The tattooed Hireling clucked his tongue. "Sure. Memory Restoration Whatever. I don't give two turds *what* you're doing, but I'll tell you *where* you're going. Camp. C-A-M-P. With this scrawny, stinky piece of nothing, and all the other nothings they've got irrigating avocados or weed whacking or whatever the heck is going on there."

Naomi shook her head and took a few steps backwards. "I'm not going with you."

Pooch raised his eyebrows at the calmness in her voice.

"Oh, man. You're going to put up a tantrum, too, little girl? What a day. First the cows. Then this disgusting, blabbering kid. Now you. Nonsense." The tattooed Hireling sighed and nudged his partner.

"Let's go. Just grab her, man. If they won't walk, we'll drag them back to the train."

Naomi's mind was buzzing. She slipped her hand in her pocket to roll the marble with her fingers. *Come, come, come.* Home was so close. How could she give up now? How could she allow herself to be dragged onto that train?

Even in the Hireling's grip, Pooch managed to wiggle. "Naomi, don't do anything stupid. Just come with us. How bad can it be? Remember, they've got goat milk at camp. Goat milk! Don't let him hurt you. Look at that beast! He's like five times your size. You don't want him to tackle you. He'll crush you."

Naomi crossed her arms. "Don't worry, Pooch. *Mick* isn't going to hurt me."

Stunned, Mick took a step back.

"What the...." The tattooed Hireling's brow scrunched up in confusion.

"How do you know Mick's name?" he fired off at Naomi.

"Ask him," Naomi said, gesturing to Mick.

The Hireling turned to Mick. "Man, how does this rodent know your name?"

Pooch licked his lips in excitement and bounced from foot to foot.

Mick's face twitched. Naomi could tell he was weighing the consequences of his arrangement with Joslyn being revealed. He was terrified of the outcome. She was sure of it.

Naomi saw an opportunity. "Mick and I know each other," she said.

The tattooed Hireling stared at Mick, waiting for an explanation.

"I was part of the Memory Restoration effort..." Mick trailed off, struggling to quickly form a lie.

"None of the brats actually opted for that foolishness," the tattooed Hireling said. "None of them got the shot. Nobody wanted their memory back."

"Nah! Naomi did!" Pooch blurted out. "She got her memory back! For real. I saw her in the canyon after they kicked her out of the camp. Her memories were just starting to come back. Real blurry. Not so sure of this or that. She didn't even know who I was, and nobody forgets me. Nobody."

"Shut up," the Hireling grumbled.

"Show him your scar," Mick commanded Naomi.

She stared at him, speechless, unsure what he was asking for.

"What scar?" she asked.

Mick grabbed Naomi by the waist, roughly pulling up her sleeve, as Pooch cried out in protest and Naomi struggled to push him away. He revealed the skin on her arm where the doctor had administered the shot.

"See?" Mick spat at his partner before letting Naomi go. "She got her memories back. She was the only one."

Naomi twisted to look at her arm, and found herself doubly shocked that, one, it hadn't even occurred to her before to examine the injection site, and two, there was a scar in the shape of the letter "H," smaller than the tip of her pinky finger.

"Headquarters," Mick emphasized, explaining the "H." "She's officially free. In fact, she's not welcome back at camp. The Director made that clear. We can't take her in. Only this guy."

"Well, how about that," his partner said. "I stand corrected."

Mick shrugged. "Still weird she knows your name, man," his partner said.

"Let's get out of here," Mick said and turned his back to Naomi. "We'll take this kid on the train to the next stop and then order a truck to bring him to the camp."

Abruptly, Pooch's Hireling began to drag him away, following Mick, who was storming back to the train. Pooch began to blabber, but Naomi couldn't make out what he was saying.

She stood in the dry creek bed, alone and free to continue on, to curl up on the ground, to throw a rock into the sky. But she kept rubbing her fingers over the H-shaped scar on her arm, watching the back of Pooch's greasy head as he bobbed away. The realization of his fate bore into her like a thorn.

Tomorrow, he wouldn't remember her. He wouldn't remember watching Naomi set herself free along the train tracks, without a scream or a punch. He wouldn't remember being starving in the Canyon or dangling Trouble out the window. He wouldn't remember being abandoned by Axe and Glitch or hopping a train alone. He wouldn't remember his mother's smile, or how he got his nickname, or his favorite bedtime story, or the nastiest joke he ever heard.

He wouldn't remember what the moon was.

"Wait!" Naomi called out. The two Hirelings and Pooch spun around.

Naomi jogged over to them. "Can I please say good-bye to my friend?"

"You've got to be kidding me," the tattooed Hireling said.

Naomi made eye contact with Mick, and the knowledge they shared passed between them. "Quickly," Mick said.

Pooch stuttered but then fell into silence, as Naomi gave him a hug and slipped her hand into his pocket. "Don't lose it," she whispered before she pulled back.

"See ya later, skater," Pooch whispered. His Hireling tugged on him, and the three of them boarded the train.

Moments later, the train came to life and carried on, back on course. Soon it became a blur, and Naomi continued on, down the creek bed, no longer with a marble in her pocket, but with the reassurance that the token that had guided her this far was exactly where it needed to be.

CHAPTER 26

The sun was melting into the horizon when Naomi heard the roar of the ocean. Now, the creek bottom was less rocky and sandier. The oaks and dry shrubs that had lined the sides of the creek were replaced with stiff reeds and dune grasses. Now, the rolling sand dunes seemed to swallow the creek bed completely.

Naomi threw herself into the cool sand. It stuck to the sweat on her face and neck. It felt like home. She allowed herself a few moments to rest there and feel the ocean breeze cool the sweat on her scalp.

Then she crawled to the top of a dune to take in the inky ocean of her memories. Even in the fading light, Naomi could see the silver spray of the crashing waves, each one bursting with fresh strength.

Naomi fought off the desire to take off her shoes and run into the dark water and let it hold her. It was home, but she was not done. She had reached the coast and now she needed to get into town. She needed to find her neighborhood and then her street. She needed to find her home and hope her family was still there.

She could see the dim lights of town. Naomi made her way in that direction.

"Careful," Papa whispers.

"She knows," Mama reassures him. "Naomi is gentle. It's okay."

Mama unfolds the crisp white blanket, revealing Eli, barely seven pounds.

"So tiny," Naomi whispers.

"Scrawny, like a chicken," Mama says. "You were the same way."

"I was?" Naomi asks. "That small?"

"Yep," Papa says. "I could hold you with one arm. Like this."

"Do it again," Naomi asks.

"You're too big, silly," Papa says.

"Please!"

Mama smiles as Papa picks up Naomi, clumsily cradling her like a baby. Naomi hollers with laughter and Eli squirms in his blanket.

"He's waking up! Put me down!" Naomi demands.

She returns to her place, hovering over Eli.

He opens his pink, toothless mouth and his eyes at the same time.

"It's normal for babies to cry," Papa warns, readying Naomi for the sounds. But Eli just croaks. His eyes shift and focus on Naomi, who leans in, inches from his face. She runs her finger along his soft cheek, covered with fuzz, and he coos and goes back to sleep.

"Oh, you're going to be a good sister," Papa says, kissing the top of her head.

The roads were empty, and many of the homes were boarded up. On each street, only a few houses were lit from the inside. Curtains were drawn.

Three streets away. Naomi's pace quickened. Daylight had faded. There was no fog in the night, but the air was thick with salty moisture.

Two streets away. Naomi's pace slowed. She tried to shut out the doubts and questions, but they were so persistent.

One street away. Naomi barely moved forward. The streets were silent. The night was silent. Naomi was silent. Home was around the corner.

"Naomi?" The voice was familiar, low and gravely. A man was sitting on the steps of his porch, smoking. He stubbed out the cigarette under his left shoe.

"Naomi, is that you?"

She stepped out of the shadowy street into the dim light cast through the dark curtain hung in the man's front window. Naomi studied the tight, tired face of a man, Joaquin, who had once worked with her father. "Yeah, it's me," she said softly.

"Oh my word," Joaquin said under his breath. "You're back. They actually let you all out? They actually did it?"

Naomi remembered that he had a son, who was likely in a Crisis Camp. She quickly shook her head. She didn't want to prolong Joaquin's disappointment.

"Not all of us," she said. "I took my memory back. So, they let me go. None of the other girls did it, though. I don't know what happened in the boys' Crisis Camp. I don't know if any of the boys got out."

The man's head dropped. He picked up the cigarette off the ground, straightened out the smashed end, and lit it again.

"I miss him," he said to the night. "All the time."

"I'm sorry," Naomi whispered and turned to go. Her home was around the corner. Her family, possibly, was around the corner. But Joaquin called her back.

"Your family got a pass to go to the Inner Desert Region. More work there, supposedly. Left this morning. Took the train. They're gone."

CHAPTER 27

Stunned, Naomi froze. If she ran, she was mere seconds away from her home. If she crawled, it would only take minutes. She was that close. But now this. Gone.

"The train?" she asked the darkness. It couldn't be. How could anything be that unfair? Naomi had been there, dozens of feet away. She imagined Eli at the window, looking out at the dry creek bed, seeing a girl moving swiftly, head down, not realizing it was his own sister. She remembered Pooch joking. What if. *What if?*

"Are you sure?" Naomi asked. "They left this morning?"

The cigarette crackled as Joaquin inhaled. "Think so," he said and coughed. "Talked to your father just days ago. Told me his plan. You go see,

149

though. If no one is at your house, you stay here tonight. That's alright. You'll stay in his room. His bed is all made up for him."

Naomi could barely stand the man's sadness.

"Okay," she mumbled and willed her feet to start moving again.

She carried on in the darkness, turned the corner, and looked down the lonely emptiness of her street. One house, boarded. Two houses, boarded. Three houses, boarded. Her home was next.

Dark.

Her home wasn't boarded up like the others, but it was dark. She walked up the path to the front door and turned the round handle. Locked. She reached under a loose slab on the porch where Mama kept an extra key. Empty. She went to each window and tried to pull up. Locked. She went to the back door and turned the knob. Locked. Curtains drawn. Not a ray of light from the inside. Not a sound.

Naomi sat on the porch. She felt a lightness, a dizziness. It was similar to what she had felt at Joslyn's after she unburdened herself of her story. But this was the lightness of defeat. Hope and purpose drained from her.

She couldn't believe it. Her family had been on the train. They had been so close. She thought about the girl in the window. Mama could have been sitting next to that girl. She could have been *right there*. If only she had gone with Pooch when he first asked, if only she had gotten on that train, if only they had moved swiftly, out of the Hirelings' sight, she probably would have found them.

If only.

A small part of her mind started churning. Make a plan. *Make a plan.* Stay at Joaquin's? Figure out how to get to the Inner Desert Region? Hop the next train? Go back to Joslyn's? She would welcome Naomi back, right? Naomi could help her on the ranch. Joslyn could be her new family. They could train Glitter.

None of it made any sense.

Naomi felt for a pull. She listened for a voice in her mind to give her direction. There was nothing. She scanned her street. A few houses were lit from the inside. Most were not. Nothing.

The energy to devise a plan fizzled. She collapsed onto her porch steps, no sense of what to do next.

Then a shriek. A high holler. Naomi listened closely. The sound broke the silence. Was it joyful? Was it celebratory? Naomi couldn't tell.

Something was pounding against aluminum. Boom. Then a holler. Boom. Then the holler again.

In the battle between defeat and curiosity, her curiosity won, and Naomi got to her feet and moved in the direction of the noise. The closer she got; she was sure: It was a shriek of joy. It sounded wildly out of place in the dark, sad neighborhood.

CHAPTER 28

It was a young child's voice, battle-crying out the words: *Take that!* Boom. The sound again of something pounding on aluminum. There was a rhythm to it. Boom. Boom. *Boom.* As she got closer, there was a new sound. Laughter. Not just any laughter. The sound of a young child's laughter. Unrestrained and boastful.

She turned the corner. More homes, boarded up. More homes, dark. But there was one home with soft orange light spilling from two windows. Naomi hesitated on the sidewalk, letting her eyes adjust. A group of people were sitting on the porch. In the driveway, two children were hitting a ball against the aluminum garage door. Boom.

Naomi paused. A memory emerged from deep inside of her.

"*Take that!*" *Eli screeches and smashes his little fist against the red, rubber ball, which smashes into the aluminum garage door, rattling the house.*

"*Do you have to do it so hard?*" *Mama yells from inside. The kitchen window is open. She is frying strips of chicken with peppers and onions. Rice is steaming.*

"*You play handball like your life depends on it,*" *Naomi teases Eli. "Why do you scream every time you hit the ball?*"

"*It's what everyone does when we play handball,*" *he says. "All the kids at school.*"

"*But why?*" *Naomi presses.*

He throws up his skinny arms, exasperated by her ignorance. "You say it to rattle your opponent."

Eli pulls a silver marble out of his pocket. He holds it up in the sunlight. "The King of Handball gets to keep this marble. It's a rare silver marble. Super rare. I reigned today at school. I was unbeatable. So, I got to keep it and take it home."

"*Well, if I win, it's mine,*" *Naomi says. She squints her eyes and sneers, playfully threating him.*

"*Good luck, sister,*" *he says. "Watch out. I'm king.*"

The game resumes. Eli hits the ball with his little fist. It smashes against the garage door, ricochets back, making a smooth arc over Naomi's head despite her best effort to intercept it.

"*Told you!*" *Eli bellows, skipping in circles. He stops and shakes his bottom at her. Naomi chases him and scoops him up, tickling his sides.*

"*Let go! Leave me alone!*" Eli screams, laughing and wiggling in her grip.

"*I love you too much to leave you,*" she whispers in his ear.

CHAPTER 29

Naomi stood in front of the house with the two lit windows. A boy with a handball tucked under his arm stared in her direction. Another boy stood behind him.

On the porch, a group of adults had stopped talking. A man stood up. He squinted in Naomi's direction, trying to see her clearly in the dark. A woman stood up. But she didn't spend a moment trying to see. She ran down the path, toward Naomi. She ran like fire was at her heels and Naomi was a pond of still water.

She crashed into Naomi, both of her arms wrapping around her, sobbing.

The boy dropped the ball. It rolled down the driveway into the empty street, and he ran toward Naomi, too, with the same ferocity. Somehow, he made his way between Naomi and the woman, sandwiched in between their warm bodies.

And then the man stood up. But he couldn't run. He stumbled, dropping to his knees, pressing his hands and face on the sidewalk.

And the other adults began chattering, cheering, and crying, like quail at dawn after a long cold night.

Naomi managed to pull herself from the bodies. She looked at the faces. Eli. Mama. Papa.

They were here, at a neighbor's house. They had not left.

Mama, Papa, Eli, and Naomi held each other.

"You were right, son," Papa whispered to Eli. "Going to the Inland Desert Region would have been a terrible idea. She loved us too much not to come back. She came back. *She came home.*"

CHAPTER 30

Naomi spent that first night back in Eli's bed. She held him until his body stopped twitching with excitement and he slept.

But she didn't sleep. She had told her family everything—about Lu and Shay, about getting her memory back, about traveling through the canyon, finding the notice, riding on Pooch's handlebars, sleeping under Joslyn's window, and Pooch getting caught at the train. She told them about the coyote-dog, which was Eli's favorite part, and he wanted to know about its dark eyes and thick fur and if Naomi thought it might come out of the canyon to be their pet.

She told them that Joslyn had said that sometimes it was easier to do the wrong thing, that often doing the right thing took wild bravery, that mistakes couldn't be unmade but that things could be made right again—there was always a way and it took courage and strength and love.

When Naomi told that part of the story, Mama sobbed and went to the kitchen window and looked east, toward the canyon. Eli asked her what she was doing, and Mama said that she was thanking Joslyn with her heart and hoping Joslyn could feel it.

Naomi told them about her hike down the dry creek bed and the wild sense of right she felt when she reached the dunes and saw the miles and miles of inky ocean in front of her. She told them about Joaquin, going to their locked, dark house, and hearing Eli play handball against the neighbor's garage door.

Then it was her family's turn to talk, but they were too tired and overwhelmed, and they said they would tell her everything in the morning, that there was much to tell, and much of it may seem hopeless, but some of it wasn't. They said the Crisis was over but life wasn't the way it used to be and that as a family they needed to figure out what they were going to do and that they would do that together, the four of them.

Mama heated a bucket of water and sat next to the tub while Naomi cleaned herself for the first time in days, scrubbing off the dust, grime, and dried blood. Mama cried when she saw Naomi's bruised hip and scabbed elbow. Her cheeks flushed with rage as she ran her fingers over Naomi's "H" scar, barely able to speak. Naomi reassured her that the scar was worth it, a small sacrifice for her freedom. Naomi told Mama about traveling to the cave, and again Mama shed tears, this time from the memory itself of taking Naomi there as a young girl, when inklings of the Crisis were creeping into their daily lives, and also because Naomi had been alone at the cave, which Mama said was rumored to be a place where disagreements had escalated to violence.

With a kitchen cup, Mama poured water over Naomi's hair and used a small dollop of precious shampoo to give Naomi a frothy, scalp massage and then ran a comb through her hair, releasing the knots. When Naomi was clean and clothed in her old pants and shirt, the family kissed and hugged and kissed and hugged their girl until she felt dizzy and parched from all their love and forgiveness, and then finally, her parents retired to their room, and Naomi laid down in Eli's bed next to him.

In the dark, she looked around the room, taking in the familiarity of Eli's few, but cherished, things. A flag their grandfather had given him. His handball. A jar of marbles. Then she saw Joslyn's backpack on the floor by the door where she had left it.

She remembered that Joslyn had put a book in the backpack, something for her to look at if she needed a break. But Naomi hadn't taken a break.

She untangled her arms from Eli's limp body, lit the thick white candle by his bed, and retrieved the book from the backpack. She expected it to be a book about pruning or medicinal herbs or pest control, but it wasn't. It was one of the thin books, one of Hanako's books. The entire book was a poem. The embossed title on the cover had been worn away. Joslyn had dog-eared a page, which Naomi immediately opened to. Several lines had been lightly underlined.

> *After all these dark times,*
> *after everything we've been through,*
> *you and I*
> *and all the others we love,*
> *and those we don't, too,*
>
> *it's the rain smell*
> *I remember most clearly*
> *when I close my eyes and try to forget.*
>
> *You know that rain smell,*
> *don't you?*
>
> *And what is it*
> *that I am most grateful for?*
>
> *That it is the rain smell*

that lingers in my memory,
not everything else.

She read the lines several times, each time feeling more like the author had written it just for her. Even in the camp, Naomi thought, without her memory, she remembered something without knowing it was what she remembered: the love of her family.

Naomi closed the book, hugged it to her chest, and rested her chin on the cover. Like Mama had, she used her heart to thank Joslyn and she hoped Joslyn could feel it. Finally, the fog horn sounded. Soon, in an hour or two, the night fog would make its way up through town, past Headquarters, up the canyon, past the railroad tracks, past Joslyn's cottage, past the broken mansion, past Outpost #5, past the cave, to Lu and Shay's tent. With her brother sleeping deeply by her right hip, with her forgiving parents resting in their bed on the other side of the wall, with the ocean roiling just blocks away, Naomi trained her thoughts on her friends in their tent, on the other children who had been stolen, including Pooch with Eli's marble in his pocket. She tried to use her thoughts to connect with them, to build a bridge between her in the warmth of Eli's bed, to them in their cold cots, separated from their own histories. *Come home. If there isn't a way, I will find a way to get to you*, she thought. *Come.*

Acknowledgments

I'm grateful that it was Deb Alix who acquired this book and coaxed me through an invigorating process of expanding the story and deepening the themes. I'm also grateful to Abby Macenka and her team for their work in making the book better and to Cherie Fox for the beautiful cover design.

I started writing this story in 2019. Since then the world has become a different place and so has the story. One thing that has remained the same is the gratitude I have for the following people:

Alison, for reading early drafts and offering valuable suggestions, but most importantly, for more than two decades of writing and friendship.

Jane, for advising me to write my way through.

Karen, Erin, and Mina, for your daily support.

Laina, Rebekah, Cindy, Naomi, Shelana, Meg, and Lisa for years of discussion about creative work and for being a part of my deep connection to coastal California, all of which informed this book.

My small family, Carol, Barbara, Jay, Laura, Leah, Jason, Becky, Rick, Bonnie, and Beverly, for being wonderful.

My nieces and nephews, Logan, Isla, Kate, Arlo, and Flynn, for being bright lights.

My grandmother, Barbara, for showing me how to tell a wild, half-true story.

My parents and my brother, for filling my childhood with love and books.

Samuel and Abel, for your ideas, questions, and love.

Scott, for our life and for being my favorite writer.

Jennifer Liss works in educational publishing and specializes in writing fiction for struggling readers. She lives in Northern California with her husband and two sons.